PENGUIN CLASSICS
Maigret's Holiday

'I love reading Simenon. He makes me think of Chekhov
— William Faulkner

'A truly wonderful writer . . . marvellously readable – lucid,
simple, absolutely in tune with the world he creates'
— Muriel Spark

'Few writers have ever conveyed with such a sure touch, the
bleakness of human life'   — A. N. Wilson

'One of the greatest writers of the twentieth century . . .
Simenon was unequalled at making us look inside, though the
ability was masked by his brilliance at absorbing us obsessively
in his stories'   — *Guardian*

'A novelist who entered his fictional world as if he were part
of it'   — Peter Ackroyd

'The greatest of all, the most genuine novelist we have had
in literature'   — André Gide

'Superb . . . The most addictive of writers . . . A unique teller
of tales'   — *Observer*

'The mysteries of the human personality are revealed in all
their disconcerting complexity'   — Anita Brookner

'A writer who, more than any other crime novelist, combined a
high literary reputation with popular appeal'   — P. D. James

'A supreme writer . . . Unforgettable vividness'   — *Independent*

'Compelling, remorseless, brilliant'   — John Gray

'Extraordinary masterpieces of the twentieth century'
— John Banville

ABOUT THE AUTHOR

Georges Simenon was born on 12 February 1903 in Liège, Belgium, and died in 1989 in Lausanne, Switzerland, where he had lived for the latter part of his life. Between 1931 and 1972 he published seventy-five novels and twenty-eight short stories featuring Inspector Maigret.

Simenon always resisted identifying himself with his famous literary character, but acknowledged that they shared an important characteristic:

> My motto, to the extent that I have one, has been noted often enough, and I've always conformed to it. It's the one I've given to old Maigret, who resembles me in certain points . . . 'understand and judge not'.

Penguin is publishing the entire series of Maigret novels.

GEORGES SIMENON

Maigret's Holiday

Translated by ROS SCHWARTZ

PENGUIN BOOKS

PENGUIN CLASSICS

UK | USA | Canada | Ireland | Australia
India | New Zealand | South Africa

Penguin Books is part of the Penguin Random House group of companies
whose addresses can be found at global.penguinrandomhouse.com.

Penguin
Random House
UK

First published in French as *Les Vacances de Maigret* by Presses de la Cité 1948
This translation first published 2016

011

The moral rights of the author and translator have been asserted
Set in Dante MT Std 12.5/15pt
Typeset by Palimpsest Book Production Limited, Falkirk, Stirlingshire
Printed and bound in Great Britain by Clays Ltd, Elcograf S.p.A.

ISBN: 978-0-141-198074-4

www.greenpenguin.co.uk

MIX
Paper from
responsible sources
FSC® C018179

Penguin Random House is committed to a
sustainable future for our business, our readers
and our planet. This book is made from Forest
Stewardship Council® certified paper.

Maigret's Holiday

1.

The street was narrow, like all the streets in the old quarter of Les Sables d'Olonne, with uneven cobblestones and pavements so narrow that you had to step off to let another person pass. The entrance to the corner building was a magnificent double door, painted a dark, rich, pristine green, with two highly polished brass knockers of the kind found only on the houses of provincial lawyers or convents.

Opposite were parked two long, gleaming cars which exuded the same aura of spotlessness and comfort. Maigret recognized them, they both belonged to surgeons.

'I could have been a surgeon too,' he thought to himself. And owned a car like that. Probably not a surgeon, but it was a fact that he had almost become a doctor. He had set out to study medicine and sometimes felt a hankering for the medical profession. If his father hadn't died three years too soon . . .

Before mounting the step, he drew his watch out of his pocket. It showed three o'clock. The same instant, the chapel's slightly shrill peal rang out, and then came the deeper chimes of Notre-Dame over the rooftops of the town's little houses.

He sighed and pressed the electric bell. He sighed because it was absurd to take his watch out of his pocket at the same time every day. He sighed because it was no less absurd to arrive on the dot of three, as if the fate of the world depended on it. He sighed because, in the time it took to wait for the click of the door, which opened automatically, soundlessly, smoothly, thanks to a well-oiled mechanism, he would, as on the previous days, become a different man.

Not even a man. His shoulders were still the broad shoulders of Detective Chief Inspector Maigret, his burly form did not diminish.

From the minute he set foot in the wide, bright corridor, however, he felt like a little boy, the young Maigret who, long ago, in his village in the Allier, used to walk on tiptoe and hold his breath when, at dawn, his hands frozen and his nose red, he entered the sacristy to don his choirboy's cassock.

The atmosphere here was reminiscent of those days. A faint pharmaceutical smell replaced the fragrance of incense, but it was not the sickening smell of hospitals, it was more complex, more refined, more *exquisite*. Underfoot was a soft linoleum the equivalent of which he had never seen anywhere. The walls too, covered with oil paint, were smoother, of a creamier white than elsewhere. Even the moistness in the air and the purity of the silence had a quality that cannot be found anywhere other than in a convent.

He instinctively turned to the right and bowed, like the choirboy walking past the altar, murmuring:

'Good afternoon, Sister . . .'

In a neat, light-filled glazed office with a window on to

the corridor, a nun wearing a cornette sat in front of a register. She smiled at him and said:

'Good afternoon, Monsieur 6 . . . I telephoned to ask if you may go up . . . Our dear patient is improving every day.'

This one was Sister Aurélie. In ordinary life, she would probably have been a woman in her fifties, but beneath her white headdress, her caramel-smooth face was ageless.

'Hello!' she said in a hushed voice. 'Is that you, Sister Marie des Anges? . . . Monsieur 6 is downstairs . . .'

Maigret did not take offence, did not even grow impatient. Goodness, how futile this daily ritual was. They were expecting him upstairs. They knew he arrived on the dot of three. He was capable of going up to the first floor all by himself.

But no! They were sticklers for routine. Sister Aurélie smiled at him, and he looked at the red-carpeted stairs where Sister Marie des Anges would appear.

She too smiled, her hands lost in the voluminous sleeves of her grey habit.

'Would you like to come up, Monsieur 6?'

He knew very well that she would whisper, as if it were a secret or a sensational piece of news:

'Our dear patient is improving every day . . .'

He walked on tiptoe. He might have blushed if, by chance, his weight had caused a stair to creak. He even turned away slightly when he spoke, to disguise the smell of Calvados which he drank every day after his lunch.

The sunlight streamed into the corridor in slanting rays, as in paintings of saints. He occasionally passed a trolley on which lay a patient being wheeled to the operating theatre and whose fixed stare was the only thing he remembered.

Sister Aldegonde invariably came to the doorway of the vast, twenty-bed ward, as if by chance, as if she had some business there, purely to say to him in passing, with a pious smile:

'Good afternoon, Monsieur 6 . . .'

Then, a little further on, Sister Marie des Anges pushed open door number 6, and stood aside.

Sitting up in bed with a strange expression on her pallid face, a woman watched him come in. It was Madame Maigret, with a look that seemed to be saying to him:

'My poor Maigret, how you have changed . . .'

Why was he still walking on tiptoe, talking in a quiet voice that wasn't his, moving cautiously as if in a china shop? He kissed her on the forehead, spotted the oranges and biscuits on the bedside table and, on the blanket, a piece of knitting that infuriated him.

'Again?'

'Sister Marie des Anges allowed me to do a little bit.'

There were other rituals, like greeting the old lady in the other bed. For they had not been able to get a single room.

'Good afternoon, Mademoiselle Rinquet . . .'

She looked at him with her darting, beady little eyes. His visits enraged her. All the time he was there, her worn-looking face maintained a surly expression.

'Sit down, my poor Maigret . . .'

She was the one who was ill. She was the one who had needed emergency surgery three days after their arrival in

Les Sables d'Olonne, where they had come to spend their holiday. But she was calling him 'my poor Maigret'.

It was much too hot, but nothing on earth would make him take off his jacket. Sister Marie des Anges popped in from time to time, goodness knows why, to move a glass of water, bring in a thermometer or some other item. Each time she would mutter, glancing at Maigret:

'Excuse me . . .'

As for Madame Maigret, every day she asked:

'What have you had to eat?'

But actually, she wasn't so far off the mark. What else was there for him to do, other than eat and drink? The fact was that he had never drunk so much in his life.

The day after the operation, the surgeon had advised:

'Don't stay longer than half an hour.'

Now it had become a routine, a ritual. He stayed for half an hour. He had nothing to say. The presence of the bad-tempered spinster inhibited him. In any case, in normal times, what did he talk about to his wife when he was with her? He was beginning to ask himself this question. Nothing, in short, was the answer. So why was he missing her so much all the time?

Here, he did nothing but wait; wait for the half-hour to come to an end. After a few minutes, Madame Maigret picked up her knitting to give an impression of composure. Since she had to put up with Mademoiselle Rinquet's presence all day and all night, she treated her with consideration. If she spoke, she would hastily add:

'Isn't that so, Mademoiselle Rinquet?'

Then she winked at Maigret. He guessed what that

meant. Women hate letting their petty anxieties show, especially Madame Maigret, and there they both were confined to bed.

'I wrote a card to my sister . . . Will you be so kind as to post it for me?'

He slipped the postcard with a picture of the convent hospital with its pretty white façade and green door into his left breast pocket.

Now for a stupid detail. Left pocket or right pocket? That question was to come back to haunt him at eleven o'clock that night.

For years and years, each of his pockets had always had a clearly defined purpose. In his left trouser pocket, his tobacco pouch and his handkerchief – so there were always wisps of tobacco in his handkerchiefs. Right pocket, his two pipes and small change. Left back pocket, his wallet, which was always stuffed with useless bits of paper and made one buttock look bigger than the other.

He never carried keys on him. Whenever he took them by mistake, he would lose them. He hardly put anything in his jacket, only a box of matches in the right-hand pocket.

That is why, when he had newspapers to take away or letters to post, he slipped them in his left breast pocket.

Had he done so that day? It was likely. He was sitting by the frosted-glass window. Sister Marie des Anges had come in a couple of times, darting a furtive glance in his direction each time. She was very young. There wasn't a crease on her rosy face.

A fool might perhaps have claimed that she was in love

with him, for she would rush to meet him on the stairs and become a butterfingers when he was in the room.

He knew very well that there was something else, something much simpler, more naive and childish.

Like the idea, which had come from her, of calling him 'Monsieur 6'. Because he dreaded people's curiosity and didn't like his name being yelled right, left and centre. He was on holiday, wasn't he, yes or no?

Did he really hate being on holiday? All year long he would sigh:

'Oh to have some peace and quiet at last, hours and hours to fill as I please . . .'

Hours completely free, days with no commitments, no meetings. In Paris, in his office at Quai des Orfèvres, that sounded like unimaginable bliss.

Was he missing Madame Maigret?

No! He knew himself. He complained. He was grumpy. But deep down, he knew that this holiday would be just like all the others. In six months, in a year's time, he would be thinking:

'My goodness! I was so happy at Les Sables d'Olonne . . .'

And with hindsight, this hospital where he felt so ill at ease would seem like a delightful place. He would melt at the memory of Sister Marie des Anges' candid, blushing face.

Never did he take his watch out before hearing the little chimes of the chapel bell signalling that it was half past three. He even pretended not to have heard. Was Madame Maigret taken in? She was the one who had to say:

'Time's up, Maigret . . .'

'I'll telephone tomorrow morning,' he would say, rising to his feet, as if this were something new.

He telephoned every morning. There was no telephone in the room, but it was Sister Aurélie, downstairs, who answered:

'Our dear patient had a very good night . . .'

Sometimes she would add:

'The chaplain will be coming later to keep her company.'

His life was as highly regulated as that of a prisoner in Fresnes jail. He hated obligations. He cursed at the thought of having to be somewhere at a specific time. But in actual fact, he himself had created a schedule that he kept to more scrupulously than a train its timetable.

At what point in the day could the note have been slipped into his pocket, his left breast pocket?

It was an ordinary sheet of glazed squared paper, probably torn out of an exercise book. The words were written in pencil, in a regular handwriting that looked to him like a woman's.

For pity's sake, ask to see the patient in room 15.

There was no signature. Only those words. He had slipped his wife's postcard into his left pocket. Had the note been there already? It was possible. He can't have thrust his hand deep inside his pocket.

But what about later, when he had posted the card in the letterbox by the covered market?

Three little words particularly irritated him: *For pity's sake*.

Why for pity's sake? If someone wanted to speak to him, it was perfectly straightforward to do so. He wasn't the pope. Anyone could approach him.

For pity's sake . . . That was in keeping with the cloying atmosphere into which he stepped every afternoon, with the nuns' faint smiles as if effaced with an eraser, with Sister Marie des Anges' little winks.

No! He shrugged. He found it hard to imagine Sister Marie des Anges slipping a note into his pocket. Even less Sister Aldegonde, who contrived to be in the corridor, opposite the public ward, whenever he walked past. As for Sister Aurélie, she was always separated from him by a window.

That was not quite true. A detail came back to him. When he had left, she had been outside her office and had shown him to the door.

Why not the elderly Mademoiselle Rinquet, for that matter? He had brushed past her bed too. And he had passed Doctor Bertrand on the stairs . . .

He didn't want to think about it. Besides, it was of no importance. It was ten thirty at night when he found the note. He had just gone up to his room at the Hôtel Bel Air. As usual, before undressing he emptied out his pockets and placed the contents on top of the chest of drawers.

As on the previous days, he had drunk a lot. Through no fault of his own. Not intentionally, but because this was the pattern his life at Les Sables d'Olonne had taken on.

For example, when he came downstairs at nine in the morning, he was forced to drink.

At eight o'clock, Julie, the smaller and darker of the two maids, brought him his coffee in bed. Why did he pretend to be asleep when he had been awake since six o'clock?

Another little habit. Holidays meant lie-ins. He rose at dawn three hundred and twenty days of the year and more, and each morning he promised himself:

'When I'm on holiday, I'm going to catch up on my sleep!'

From his room he had a view of the ocean. It was August. He slept with the windows open. The old, heavy, red-silk curtains did not meet and he was dragged from his sleep by the sun and the sound of the breakers on the sand.

And then there was the noise from the lady in number 3, next door, who had four children aged between six months and eight years, who all slept in her room.

For an hour there was shrieking, wailing, comings and goings; he could picture her, half-dressed, wearing slippers on her bare feet, her hair dishevelled, struggling with her tetchy brood, plonking one down in a corner, another on the bed, slapping the eldest who was crying, looking for the girl's lost shoe, despairing of ever getting the spirit stove, to work so she could heat up the baby's bottle. The smell of meths seeped under the communicating door to Maigret's room.

As for the elderly couple on his right, that was another performance. They talked nonstop in a monotone, their voices indistinguishable from one another, and it almost sounded as if they were reciting psalms.

Maigret had to wait until the bathroom for their floor was free, listen out for the sound of the sink draining or the toilet being flushed. He had a little balcony. He lingered there in his dressing gown, and the view was really magnificent, the vast, dazzling beach, the sea dotted with blue and white sails. He saw the first striped beach umbrellas being planted, and the first kids arriving in their red swimming costumes.

By the time he went downstairs, freshly shaven, traces of soap behind his ears, he was on his third pipe.

What was it that prompted him to go behind the scenes? Nothing. He could, like everyone else, have gone out via the sunlit dining room, which Germaine, the plump maid with incredible breasts, was busy polishing.

But no. He pushed open the door to the staff dining room and then that of the kitchen. At that moment, the bespectacled Madame Léonard was discussing the menu with the chef. Monsieur Léonard would invariably emerge from the wine cellar. At any hour of the day, he could be seen coming up from the cellar, and yet he was fairly sober.

'Beautiful day, inspector . . .'

Monsieur Léonard was in slippers and shirt-sleeves. There were peas, freshly grated carrots, leeks and potatoes in bowls. Blood from the meats ran on to the deal table, while sole and turbot lay waiting to be scaled.

'A little glass of white wine, inspector?'

The first of the day. A little drink with the owner. It was in fact an excellent local wine with a greenish tinge.

Maigret could hardly go and sit on the beach among all the mothers. He strolled along the promenade, Le Remblai, pausing from time to time. He gazed at the sea, at the swelling number of brightly clad figures playing in the waves close to the shore. Then, when he reached the town centre, he turned right into a narrow street which led to the covered market.

He wandered from stall to stall as slowly and methodically as if he had forty people to feed. He stopped in front of the fish, which were still quivering, then he lingered in front of the shellfish and proffered a matchstick to a lobster which snatched it with its pincer.

Second glass of white wine. Because just opposite was a little café where you went down one step and it was like an extension of the market, filled with mouth-watering smells.

Then he walked past Notre-Dame to go and buy his newspaper. Could he go back up to his room to read it?

He went back to the promenade and sat at the terrace of a café, always in the same place. He always dithered too, keeping the waiter standing there ready to take his order. As if he were going to drink anything else!

'A white wine.'

It had come about by chance. He would sometimes go for months without drinking white wine.

At eleven o'clock, he went inside the café to telephone the hospital, to hear Sister Aurélie say in her syrupy voice:

'Our dear patient had an excellent night.'

He had organized a series of little halts where he would sit at set times. In the hotel dining room too, he had his special corner, by the window, opposite the table of his two elderly neighbours.

On the first day, after his coffee, he had ordered a glass of Calvados. Since then Germaine invariably asked him:

'Calvados, inspector?'

He didn't dare refuse. He felt drowsy. The sun was scorching. At times the asphalt on the promenade melted underfoot and car tyres left their imprint on it.

He went up to his room for a nap, not in the bed but in the armchair which he had dragged on to the balcony, where he sat with a newspaper spread over his face.

For pity's sake, ask to see the patient in room 15 . . .

Anyone seeing him ensconced in his various favourite spots at different times of day would think he had been there for years, like the afternoon card players. But it was only nine days since he and his wife had arrived. On the first evening, they had eaten mussels. It was a treat they had been promising themselves since Paris: to eat a huge dish of freshly caught mussels.

They had both been ill. They had kept their neighbours awake. The next day, Maigret felt better, but on the beach Madame Maigret complained of vague pains. The second night, she had a fever. They still thought it was nothing serious.

'It was silly of me. I've never been able to eat mussels . . .'

Then, the following day, she was in so much pain that they had had to call Doctor Bertrand and he had sent her straight to hospital. Those few hours had been difficult, chaotic, to-ing and fro-ing, new faces, X-rays, tests.

'I assure you, doctor, it was the mussels,' repeated Madame Maigret with a wan smile.

But the doctors were not smiling. They took Maigret to one side. Acute appendicitis with the risk of peritonitis. His wife needed emergency surgery.

He paced up and down the long corridor during the operation, at the same time as a young man waiting for his wife to give birth, who had bitten his nails until his fingers bled.

That was how he had become 'Monsieur 6'.

In six days, a man develops new habits, learns to walk quietly, to smile sweetly at Sister Aurélie, and then at Sister Marie des Anges. He even learns to give a forced smile to the loathsome Mademoiselle Rinquet.

After which someone takes advantage of the situation to slip a stupid note into his pocket.

And first of all, who was the patient in room 15? Madame Maigret would know, for sure. They all knew one another even though they didn't meet. They all knew one another's business. She sometimes told her husband the gossip, discreetly, in a low voice, like in church.

'Apparently the lady in room 11 who's so kind and so gentle . . . poor thing . . . Come closer . . .'

She stammered under her breath:

'Breast cancer . . .'

Then she glanced over at Mademoiselle Rinquet's bed and fluttered her eyelashes, indicating that her fellow patient had cancer too.

'If you could have seen the pretty little girl they brought into the ward . . .'

She meant the public ward, for in fact there were three classes, as for trains: the public ward, which was like the third class, then the two-bed rooms and, finally, the first-class private rooms.

What was the point of worrying about it? All this was childish. There was really something infantile about the atmosphere in the hospital. Weren't the nuns rather child-like?

The patients too, with their petty jealousies and their whispered secrets, the sweets they hoarded like misers and the way they lay listening out for footsteps in the corridors.

For pity's sake . . .

Those three words suggested that the note could only have come from a woman. Why would the patient in room 15 need him? He did not intend to take the note seriously or ask Sister Aurélie's permission to visit someone whose name he didn't even know.

On the beach and in town, the sunshine was overpowering. At certain times, the air literally quivered with the heat and when you suddenly stepped into a puddle of shade, for a moment you could only see red.

Right! His siesta was over; it was time for him to fold up his newspaper, put on his jacket, light a pipe and go downstairs.

'See you later, inspector!'

And so it went on, hellos and goodbyes like benedictions, all day long. Everyone was pleasant, smiling. He was the only one to become disgruntled. A nice downpour or an argument with someone cantankerous would have made him feel better.

The green door and the three o'clock chimes. He wasn't even capable of not taking his watch out of his pocket!

'Good afternoon, Sister . . .'

Why didn't he genuflect, while he was about it? And now the other one – there was Sister Marie des Anges waiting for him on the stairs.

'Good afternoon, Sister . . .'

And Monsieur 6 tiptoed into Madame Maigret's room.

'How are you?'

She forced herself to sound cheerful but only managed a half-smile.

'You shouldn't have brought me oranges. I still have some left.'

'Now, you who know all the patients . . .'

Why was she signalling to him? He turned towards Mademoiselle Rinquet's bed. The old spinster lay there facing the wall, her head buried in her pillow.

He asked quietly:

'Is something wrong?'

'It's not her . . . Shh . . . Come closer . . .'

She was being very secretive. It was like being in a girls' boarding school.

'Someone died last night . . .'

She was keeping one eye on Mademoiselle Rinquet, whose blanket twitched.

'It was terrible, we could hear the screams . . . Then the family arrived . . . It went on for more than three hours. There were comings and goings . . . Several patients panicked . . . Especially when the chaplain administered the extreme unction . . . They turned the lights out in the corridor, but everyone knew . . .'

In a whisper, Madame Maigret added, jerking her head in the direction of her fellow patient:

'She thinks it's her turn next.'

Maigret didn't know what to say. He sat there, heavy and clumsy, in a foreign world.

'She was a young woman . . . A very pretty young thing, apparently . . . in room 15 . . .'

She wondered why he knitted his bushy eyebrows and automatically took a pipe out of his pocket which he didn't actually fill.

'Are you sure it was 15?'

'Of course . . . Why? . . .'

'No reason.'

He went and sat in his chair. There was no point telling Madame Maigret about the note, she would immediately become alarmed.

'What have you had to eat today?'

Mademoiselle Rinquet began to cry. Her face was hidden, only her sparse hair could be seen on the pillow, but the blanket was heaving fitfully.

'You shouldn't stay too long.'

In his robust state of health, he was visibly out of place among the sick and the silent, gliding nuns.

Before leaving, he asked:

'Do you know her name?'

'Who?'

'The girl . . . In number 15 . . .'

'Hélène Godreau . . .'

Only then did he notice that Sister Marie des Anges was red-eyed and seemed resentful towards him. Was she the person who had slipped the note in his pocket?

He felt unable to ask her. All this was so far removed from his normal world, from the dusty corridors of the Police Judiciaire, from the people he questioned in his office, sitting them down in front of him, his eyes boring into theirs at length and then bombarding them with harsh questions.

What was more, this was none of his business. A girl was dead. And then what? Someone had slipped a meaningless message into his pocket . . .

He continued on his path, like a circus horse. In short, his days were spent going round in circles exactly like a circus horse. Now, for example, it was time for the Brasserie du Remblai. He went there as if going to an important meeting, whereas in fact he had absolutely no business there.

The café was vast and bright. By the bay windows overlooking the beach and the sea sat most of the customers whom he did not even bother to glance at, strangers, holidaymakers, who had no routine, whom one did not expect to see at the same table every day.

At the back, in a spacious corner behind the billiard table, it was a different matter, with two tables around which sat a group of earnest, taciturn men, under the eye of a waiter attentive to the slightest signal from them.

They were important men, the rich, the elders. Some of them had seen the café being built and others had known Les Sables d'Olonne before the construction of Le Remblai.

Each afternoon, they gathered to play bridge. Each afternoon, they shook hands in silence, or exchanged a few short, ritual words.

They had already grown accustomed to the presence of Maigret, who did not play cards but straddled a chair and watched them play, smoking his pipe and sipping a white wine.

They usually waved to him by way of a greeting. Only Monsieur Mansuy, the chief inspector of police, who had introduced him to these men, stirred himself to get up and shake his hand.

'Is your wife continuing to improve?'

He answered yes, without thinking. He also added, without thinking:

'A girl died last night, at the hospital . . .'

He had spoken softly, but even so his voice boomed, especially in the silence that reigned over the two tables.

He realized from the gentlemen's reaction that he had committed a blunder. Chief Inspector Mansuy signalled to him not to say any more.

Although he had been watching them play for six days, he still hadn't managed to understand the game. This time, he contented himself with watching their faces.

Monsieur Lourceau, the ship-owner, was very old, but tall, still strong, with a ruddy face beneath a crown of white hair. He was the best bridge player of all of them and, when his partner made a mistake, he had a way of glaring at him that did not make one want to play with him.

Depaty, the estate agent, who handled mainly private homes and housing developments, was livelier, with mischievous eyes that belied his seventy years.

Then there was a building contractor, a judge, a boat-builder and the deputy mayor.

The youngest player must have been between forty-five and fifty. He was just finishing a game. He was thin and wiry, with sharp eyes and lustrous brown hair, and he dressed with studied elegance, if not with affectation.

When he had played his last card, he stood up, as he usually did, and went over to the telephone booth. Maigret glanced up at the clock. It was four thirty. Each day, at the same time, that player made a telephone call.

Chief Inspector Mansuy, who changed places with his neighbour for the next game, leaned towards his colleague and murmured:

'It's his sister-in-law who died . . .'

The man who telephoned his wife every day during the game was Doctor Bellamy. He lived less than three hundred metres away, the big white house after the casino, exactly halfway between the casino and the pier, in one of the town's most beautiful residences. It could be seen from the bay window. With its calm dignity, the immaculate, even façade with its big, high windows was reminiscent of the convent hospital.

Doctor Bellamy was walking back, impassive, to the table where the others were waiting for him and the cards had already been dealt. Monsieur Lourceau, who did not like futile questions to interrupt the solemnity of bridge, gave a shrug. Things had probably gone on like this for years.

The doctor was not a man to allow himself to be intimidated. Not a muscle in his face moved. He scanned his hand at a glance, and called:

'Two clubs . . .'

Then, during the game, he began for the first time to examine Maigret covertly. It was barely noticeable. His glances were so fleeting that Maigret only just intercepted them in passing.

For pity's sake . . .

Why were words forming unconsciously in Maigret's mind that would then nag away at him during the rest of the game? *In any case, there is one man who won't have any pity . . .*

He had rarely seen eyes that were so hard and at the same time blazing, a man so in control of himself, so capable of betraying nothing of his feelings.

On previous days, Maigret had not waited for the game of bridge to end. Other 'corners' awaited him. He was horrified at the thought of the slightest change to his routine.

'Will you still be here at six o'clock?' he asked Chief Inspector Mansuy.

The latter looked at his watch, a pointless action, before replying that he would.

Le Remblai, right to the end of the promenade this time, past Doctor Bellamy's house, which was typical of those residences that passers-by gaze at with envy, saying:

'It must be so lovely to live there . . .'

Then the port, the yacht-builder's yard with its sails spread over the pavement, the ferryman, the boats coming in and mooring alongside each other opposite the fish market.

Here, there was a little café painted green, with four steps, a dark bar, two or three tables covered with brown oilcloth and nothing but men wearing blue, their high rubber waders turned down over their thighs.

'A small glass of white wine . . .'

. . .Which did not taste the same as the wine at the Hôtel Bel Air, or that of the covered market, or the white wine at the Brasserie du Remblai.

Now all he had to do was to walk to the end of the quayside, then turn right and make his way back through the narrow streets where the single-storey houses were teeming with life, noise and smells.

When, at six o'clock, he reached the Brasserie du Remblai, Chief Inspector Mansuy, who had just emerged, stood winding up his watch as he waited for Maigret.

2.

It took half an hour, and the wait was not unpleasant, on the contrary. Chief Inspector Mansuy had said to him:

'I have to stop by the police station. I need to sign some documents and there's probably a man waiting to see me.'

He was a stocky redhead, and there was an air of formality, of shyness even, about him – he always seemed to be saying 'I'm sorry, but I assure you I'm doing everything I can.'

As a child he had probably been one of those pretentious boys who spend their break time daydreaming in a corner, and are described as being too serious for their age. He was a bachelor and lived in furnished lodgings owned by a widow, in a house near the Hôtel Bel Air. From time to time, he came to have an aperitif at the hotel, and that was how Maigret had met him.

He did not seem like a proper inspector, and the police station did not seem like a proper police station either. The offices were in a residential house, on a little square. In some rooms, the wallpaper hadn't been changed, and you could tell which rooms had formerly been bedrooms, or bathrooms, with lighter patches on the walls in the shape of each piece of furniture, and pipes that had been sealed off.

But there was the smell, which Maigret sniffed with

delight, almost relief – a lovely, heavy smell, so thick you could cut through it with a knife, the odour of the leather shoulder holsters, the wool of the uniforms, administrative forms, pipes gone cold and, lastly, the poor wretches who had worn out their trouser seats on the two wooden benches in the waiting room.

Compared with the Police Judiciaire, the place appeared rather amateurish. The men gave the impression they were playing at being cops. An officer in shirt-sleeves was washing his hands and face in the courtyard. You could hear the hens in the next-door garden clucking. Other officers were playing cards in the guardroom, lounging around in imitation of real officers, and there were some very young ones who looked like conscripts.

'May I show you the way?'

The stocky chief inspector was secretly thrilled to be showing a famous name like Maigret around his station. Thrilled and a little anxious. In a spacious office, two inspectors were perched on the tables, smoking. One of them had his hat pushed back, like in American films.

Mansuy greeted them distractedly, opened the door to his office, then retraced his steps.

'No news?'

'We've kept Polyte for you . . . The sub-prefect requested that you telephone him . . .'

It was a glorious day. Since he had been at Les Sables d'Olonne, Maigret had not had a single day of rain. The windows were open, allowing the sounds of the town to filter in, and families could be seen wending their way back from the beach.

When Polyte was brought in, he was handcuffed to make it look as if the police were doing their job. He was a pathetic wretch, of indeterminate age, the sort you find at least one of in every village, shaggy, bedraggled, with a gaze that is both innocent and sly.

'In trouble again, Polyte? I imagine that this time you won't deny it?'

Polyte didn't move, didn't reply, staring docilely at Mansuy, who was slightly intimidated by the presence of the famous Maigret and was keen to impress him.

'You won't deny it, I imagine?'

He had to repeat his question twice before obtaining any kind of response from the vagrant. A nod.

'What does that mean? That you confess?'

He shook his head.

'You deny having broken into Madame Médard's garden?'

Heavens, this was comforting! Maigret felt so much more at home here than among the nuns. Polyte must be a regular. He lived in a wooden shack on the outskirts of the town, with a wife and seven or eight lice-ridden brats.

That same morning, he had turned up at a second-hand goods dealer's and tried to sell him two pairs of almost new sheets, as well as towels and women's clothing. The second-hand dealer pretended to be interested and alerted the police officer standing watch on the corner of the street, and Polyte had been arrested before he had gone two hundred metres. As for Madame Médard, the victim of the theft, she was already at the police station.

'You broke into her garden, where she had left some

27

washing out to dry . . . This isn't the first time you've jumped over her hedge . . . Last week you opened the door of her hutch and took her two biggest rabbits.'

'I never stole her rabbits—'

'She formally identified one of the skins found at your place.'

'It's my job to collect rabbit skins.'

'Even if the meat is still inside them?'

There was nothing to be done, no matter how many questions the red-cheeked Mansuy put to him, no matter how many times he tried to trip him up.

'This man sold me the linen.'

'Where?'

'In the street.'

'Which street?'

'Over there . . .'

'What's his name?'

'Don't know . . .'

'Had you seen him before?'

'Don't think so . . .'

'And he came up to you to sell you sheets and blouses?'

'I told you before . . .'

'You realize the judge won't believe you and will come down hard on you?'

'That will be unfair . . .'

Polyte gave off a smell that was reminiscent of a Salvation Army shelter, only more pungent. He was obstinate. It was clear that even if the interrogation went on for hours, he would give away nothing more, and his shrewd little eyes seemed to be saying:

'You see this isn't getting you anywhere!'

Two officers finally led him away, still handcuffed, leaving Maigret alone with the chief inspector, the windows open, the station almost empty, apart from the men in the guardroom.

'There you are! . . . That's a bit different from the cases you're used to dealing with, isn't it? . . . Here I have the time to play bridge nearly every afternoon.'

'You won't forget to telephone the sub-prefect?'

'To invite myself to dinner tomorrow, I already know what it's about . . . Have you met him? . . . A charming man . . . Earlier on you were talking to me about Philippe Bellamy . . . What do you think of him? . . . He's a character, isn't he? . . . I only transferred to Les Sables d'Olonne two years ago, but I've had time to get to know everyone . . . You've seen the main local characters . . . Some of them are quite colourful . . . Doctor Bellamy outclasses them all . . . Do you know that he's very distinguished in his field? . . . I happened to mention him to a friend, who's a doctor in Bordeaux . . . Bellamy is one of today's foremost neurologists . . . For a long time he was a consultant in a Paris hospital, where he took his teaching exams . . . He could have been made professor in a top university . . . But instead he chose to live here, with his mother . . .'

'Does his family come from Les Sables d'Olonne?'

'They've been here for several generations. You haven't met the mother, Madame Bellamy? A fairly stout, stocky old lady who walks with a stick that she wields like a sabre! . . . Once a week or so she has a run-in with the market women.'

'What did the girl die of?'

'I'm certain that the sub-prefect has invited me to dinner to discuss that very subject . . . He telephoned me this morning about it . . . He is in contact, naturally, with Doctor Bellamy . . . They see each other quite frequently.'

It relaxed him to puff gently away on his pipe as he paced up and down the office, pausing by the window from time to time, framed against the square of light, and chatting casually in languid little snippets.

'Unsurprisingly, people are talking a great deal about the accident . . . I'm surprised you haven't heard . . .'

'I know so few people here . . .'

'It was . . . let me think . . . two days ago . . . Yes, the 3rd of August . . . The report must still be in my secretary's office, but I wouldn't know where to lay my hands on it . . . Doctor Bellamy had driven to La Roche-sur-Yon, with his sister-in-law . . .'

'How old was she?'

'Nineteen . . . A strange girl, interesting-looking rather than pretty . . . Now don't start getting ideas, whatever you do . . . Lili Godreau was sweet, but her sister – whom Bellamy married – is one of the most beautiful women you'll ever come across . . . Unfortunately, you won't get much opportunity to see her, since she rarely leaves the house . . .'

'How old is she?' repeated Maigret.

'Around twenty-five . . . Bellamy's love for his wife is almost legendary around here . . . It's a real passion and everyone will tell you that he is fiercely jealous . . . Some people say that he locks her inside the house when he goes out, like for example when he comes every afternoon to play cards . . . I think they're exaggerating . . . On the other hand, Bellamy's mother never seems to be away from the house at the same time as her son and I wouldn't be surprised if she stays at home to keep an eye on her daughter-in-law. You saw the doctor telephone . . . He can't be away from home for two hours without calling her, without making contact with her, perhaps to check that she's there . . .'

'What sort of family is she from?'

'Well, her mother's life isn't exactly reassuring for a husband . . . Does this really interest you? I'll try and tell you what I know . . . Bellamy's wife is called Odette and her maiden name is Godreau . . . Her mother was from a fairly good family, the daughter of a naval officer, I think . . . She was, and still is, a very beautiful woman.

'For twenty years, at Les Sables d'Olonne, her name was a byword for sin . . . I don't know whether you've lived in a provincial town and whether you know what I'm talking about . . . She wasn't married . . . She was a kept woman . . . She was the mistress of two or three rich gentlemen in succession, including Monsieur Lourceau, whom you saw at the café . . . Curtains twitched when she walked past, lustful schoolboys and married men would turn around to gaze at her. When she entered a shop, conversations would stop and the ladies would put on a tight-lipped air . . .

'She had two daughters, said to be from different fathers, Odette and Lili . . .

'Odette grew into a young woman even more stunning

than her mother had been, and Doctor Bellamy met her before she had even reached twenty . . .

'He married her.

'You saw him. I told you he was a character. He married the young lady, but he didn't want the mother-in-law around. He gave her an allowance so that she'd leave town . . . Apparently she lives in Paris now with a retired industrialist . . .

'Since there was a younger sister, who was thirteen at the time they got married, the doctor took responsibility for her . . . He brought her up . . . Today, or rather yesterday, she was nineteen . . .

'The two of them went to La Roche-sur-Yon in Bellamy's car . . .'

'With Odette?'

'No, alone . . . Lili was a pianist and went to all the concerts . . . There was one on at La Roche-sur-Yon at four o'clock . . . Her brother-in-law drove her there . . . On the way back—'

'At what time?'

'Just after seven . . . It was still broad daylight . . . The road was far from empty . . . I'm telling you all this because it's important . . . The door, which probably hadn't been closed properly, swung open and Lili Godreau was flung on to the road . . . The car was going very fast . . . The doctor is in the habit of speeding but the gendarmes, who know him, turn a blind eye . . .'

'In other words, an accident . . .'

'An accident . . .'

Chief Inspector Mansuy faltered, almost corrected

himself, even opened his mouth. Maigret watched him with curiosity. But he repeated:

'An accident, yes.'

'It couldn't possibly be otherwise, could it?'

'I don't think so.'

'As you said earlier, it is hard to imagine that Bellamy could have had intimate relations with his sister-in-law?'

'He's not that sort of person.'

'Were there any other cars in the vicinity?'

'There was a delivery van a hundred metres behind the car . . . We questioned the driver. He didn't notice anything unusual . . . The doctor's car overtook him at top speed and, a few moments later, he saw the door swing open and someone fly out on to the tarmac . . .'

If the stocky inspector with a large head had known Maigret better, he would have noticed the change that had come over the latter during the last few minutes. Earlier, he had still been a slightly irresolute, large man puffing half-heartedly on his pipe and gazing about him with a bored expression.

But now he was somehow more substantial. His footsteps were heavier, his movements more deliberate.

Lucas, for example, who knew the chief better than anyone, would have understood at once and been delighted.

'I'll see you tomorrow, no doubt?' grunted Maigret, extending his big paw.

Mansuy was disconcerted. He had been expecting to leave with Maigret and walk part of the way with him, perhaps for them to have a drink together. Maigret was ditching him here, in his office, where he had been so pleased to do the honours and where there was nothing to detain him further. Awkwardly he picked his hat up from the table suggesting that he too was ready to leave.

'You're forgetting to telephone the sub-prefect,' Maigret reminded him.

Without irony. He wasn't doing it on purpose, his mind was elsewhere, that was all. To be more precise, he was thinking. Or to be even more precise, he was stirring up images that were still hazy.

In the doorway, he turned round.

'Had it been possible to question the girl?'

'No. She was in a coma up until her death, which occurred last night. She had a fractured skull.'

'Who was treating her?'

'Doctor Bourgeois.'

And, on the very day of her death, her brother-in-law had gone, as usual, and played bridge at the Brasserie du Remblai.

It was vague. Although Maigret was already heavier, he wasn't yet in a trance, as they called it at Quai des Orfèvres. He followed the pavement, turned left, and ended up going into a bar where he hadn't yet set foot and which would probably be added to his collection of daily watering holes.

'A white wine . . . No . . . Something dry . . .'

For pity's sake . . . said the note that someone had slipped into his pocket.

What would have happened if he had found the note

earlier, if he'd gone straight to the hospital and demanded to see patient 15? Hadn't Lili Godreau been in a coma?

He went and sat in his favourite corner at the hotel. Before going upstairs, he had to have a drink with Monsieur Léonard.

'Do you know Doctor Bellamy?'

'He's an extraordinary man . . . He treated my wife for her headaches, four years ago now. And he wouldn't accept any payment . . . I had a tough job getting him to accept a bottle of vintage chartreuse that I was saving for a special occasion . . .'

He slept, woke, reacquainted himself with the familiar sounds, the breakers on the sand, the baby bawling in the adjacent room, then the cacophony of the four children arguing with their mother and the droning of the elderly couple on his right.

Nothing had been set in motion yet, nothing, but, like the previous evening, there was a little more heaviness about him, and a haze in his mind.

White wine with the owner.

'Do you know when the funeral is?'

'You mean the Godreau girl? . . . It's tomorrow . . . At least it's scheduled for tomorrow . . . Between you and me, in confidence, I think there'll be an autopsy . . . A mere precaution, you understand? . . . Or rather to put a stop to malicious gossip . . . People are even saying it's Doctor Bellamy who suggested it . . .'

All morning, as he did his daily round going from bar to bar, he fumed a little, and it was the nuns that made him so angry.

Because if they hadn't been nuns, he would have gone and rung the hospital bell. He would have asked specific questions. It wouldn't have taken him long to find out who had slipped a piece of paper into his pocket.

But he had to wait until three o'clock. Disturbing Sister Aurélie would get him nowhere. On what grounds, anyway? Because he wanted to see his wife? He was only allowed his eleven o'clock telephone call and it was already a huge privilege that he had obtained to be allowed to go and visit Madame Maigret every afternoon.

Later, he would have to walk with muffled steps and talk in hushed tones.

'We'll soon see,' he growled after his third white wine.

All the same, at three o'clock there he was, waiting a few seconds for the church bells to ring before pressing the bell on the green door.

'Good afternoon, Monsieur 6 . . . Our dear patient is expecting you . . .'

He could hardly scowl at Sister Aurélie, and he began to smile despite himself.

'Just a moment, I'll announce you . . . I'll announce you . . .'

And the other one, Sister Marie des Anges, came to meet him at the top of the stairs. He couldn't talk to her in the corridor with all the doors open.

'Good afternoon, Monsieur 6 . . . Our dear patient . . .'

It was like a conjuring trick in which he played the conjuror's ball. He hadn't had a chance to open his mouth when he found himself in his wife's room where the horrid Mademoiselle Rinquet was staring at him with her beady little eyes.

'What's the matter with you, Maigret?'

'Me? Nothing . . .'

'You're not in a good mood . . .'

'Yes I am . . .'

'It's time for me to get out of here, isn't it? Admit that you're bored . . .'

'How are you?'

'Better . . . Doctor Bertrand thinks he'll be able to remove my staples on Monday . . . This morning, I was allowed a little chicken . . .'

He couldn't even whisper to her. How would that look? The vixen in the other bed was all ears.

'By the way, you forgot to leave me a little money . . .'

'What for?'

'A young patient came by earlier collecting contributions . . .'

A glance over at Mademoiselle Rinquet, as if he was meant to understand what was only half said. But understand what? Was she collecting money for the elderly spinster?

'What do you mean?'

'For the wreath . . .'

And for a moment, he wondered naively what the wreath had to do with the patient who was still alive. It was stupid. But he wasn't spending all his time, day in and day out, in this atmosphere of whispered secrets and meaningful looks.

'Number 15 . . .'

'Oh! Yes . . .'

Madame Maigret's exquisite tact! Because her neighbour was seriously ill, because she had cancer – and so was going to die – she thoughtfully lowered her voice to talk about the wreath!

'She's going to come back . . . Give her twenty francs . . . Almost everyone gave twenty francs . . . The funeral's tomorrow . . .'

'I know . . .'

'What did you have for lunch?'

Every day, he had to give her a detailed account of everything he had eaten.

'You haven't been served any more mussels, I hope?'

Sister Marie des Anges came in.

'May I?'

It was to introduce the young patient who was collecting money for the wreath. Maigret held out his twenty francs, together with a pencil.

'Do you want to write my wife's name, Sister?'

Sister Marie des Anges took the pencil without hesitation. Then there was a short pause. She looked up at Maigret's face and her cheeks turned a little pinker.

She wrote the surname, while he scrutinized the letters she traced on the sheet of paper. She didn't take the trouble to disguise her handwriting. Besides, her eyes had already confessed.

Visibly shaken, she withdrew, saying thank you and leading the young patient by the hand.

'Here, we really are like a family,' Madame Maigret was saying affectionately. 'You can't imagine the closeness that develops between people who are sick.'

He didn't want to contradict her, even though he was thinking of Mademoiselle Rinquet.

'I think they'll allow me home in eight or ten days . . . The day after tomorrow, they'll let me sit in an armchair for an hour.'

It wasn't very kind towards Madame Maigret, but the half-hour seemed even longer than on the other days.

'Wouldn't you like to move to a different room?'

She was horrified. How could he be so tactless as to say something like that in front of Mademoiselle Rinquet?

'Why would you want me to move?'

'I don't know . . . There must be a single room free now . . .'

Madame Maigret's alarm became more personal and she stammered, unable to believe her ears:

'Number 15? . . . Don't even think of it, Maigret!'

A room in which a girl had just died! He didn't press her. Mademoiselle Rinquet must take him for a monster. But he had merely seen it as a way of getting to speak to Sister Marie des Anges on her own.

Too bad! He'd find another way. In the corridor, as she was showing him out, he said to her:

'May I speak to you for a moment in the parlour?'

She knew what it was about and she was just as alarmed as Madame Maigret had been.

'The rules don't permit . . .'

'You mean the rules don't permit me to have a conversation with you?'

'Except in the presence of the mother superior, to whom you must make a request . . .'

'And where can I find the mother superior?'

He had inadvertently raised his voice. He was on the point of growing angry.

'Shhh . . .'

Sister Aldegonde poked her head around a half-open door and watched them from a distance.

'Can I at least talk to you here?'

'Shhh . . .'

'Can you write to me?'

'The rules don't—'

'And I presume the rules don't permit you to go into town?'

That was too much. He was verging on blasphemy.

'Listen, Sister—'

'I beg you, Monsieur 6—'

'You know what I want to—'

'Shhh . . . For goodness' sake!'

And she joined her hands, advancing and forcing him to retreat. She said out loud, no doubt for the benefit of Sister Aldegonde, who was still listening:

'I assure you that your dear patient is lacking for nothing and that she's in excellent spirits . . .'

It was pointless insisting. He was already on the stairs, on Sister Aurélie's territory now. All that remained was for him to go downstairs and leave.

'Good afternoon, Monsieur 6,' said a mellow voice behind the window. 'Will you be telephoning tomorrow?'

He felt like a great oafish boy surrounded by a gaggle of little girls who were making fun of him. Little girls of all ages, including Mademoiselle Rinquet, whom he had taken a dislike to, heaven knows why! Including Madame Maigret, who was becoming rather too much part of the place.

What point would there have been, since he couldn't talk to anyone, in writing a note to alert him?

For a good ten minutes, he railed inwardly against Sister Marie des Anges.

A hypocrite too. That tone of voice in which she'd said, to pull the wool over Sister Aldegonde's eyes:

'I assure you that your dear patient is lacking for nothing and that . . .'

And the other one, number 15, no doubt she had been a 'dear patient' too?

He walked in the shade, then in the sun, going from one street to the next and, gradually, he calmed down and saw the funny side.

Poor Sister Marie des Anges! In short, she had done what she could. She had even shown daring and initiative. What would have been an ordinary gesture anywhere else was true heroism in that place.

It wasn't her fault that Maigret had got there too late, or that the Godreau girl had died too soon.

Right now, what could he do? Go back to the hospital, ask to see the mother superior, and say: 'I need to speak to Sister Marie des Anges'?

On what grounds? What business was it of his? Here, he wasn't Maigret from the Police Judiciaire, but plain Monsieur 6.

Talk to Doctor Bellamy? To tell him what, for goodness' sake? Besides, hadn't the doctor himself insisted on having an autopsy performed on his sister-in-law?

The previous day, Chief Inspector Mansuy had told him that Lili Godreau had not regained consciousness and that she had been in a coma from the time of the accident until her death.

A nice glass of white wine was what he needed. In a real bar full of rowdy men. With real sunshine coming through the windows and not that nauseating, subdued hospital light.

As for the note, he tore it into shreds. Then he headed for the Brasserie du Remblai. Would Doctor Bellamy come for his game of cards? That was his business. When there's a death in the house, the women begin by declaring in a pitiful voice:

'No . . . Don't press me . . . I couldn't eat a thing . . . I'd rather die . . .'

Then, a little later, they are at the table asking for dessert, if they aren't exchanging recipes with their sisters-in-law.

As for Doctor Bellamy, he carried on playing bridge. He was there, just like any other day. Several times he looked at Maigret and his gaze was very sharp, very penetrating.

His eyes seemed to be saying: 'I know you're curious about me, that you are trying to understand me . . . I am not bothered in the least . . .'

No, that was not entirely true. He was bothered and, as time went by, Maigret could see that he was.

There was something else between him and the doctor, a very subtle bond, but a bond all the same.

When Maigret went somewhere and was recognized, he

was used to seeing people stare at him with curiosity, because of his reputation. Some felt compelled to ask him questions, which were generally rather stupid, or flattering.

'So tell me, inspector, what is your method?'

The cleverest ones, or the most pretentious, would declare:

'It seems to me that you are of the Bergsonian school, you follow your hunches . . .'

Some, like Lourceau and a few of the persons present, were content to see what a chief inspector from the Police Judiciaire looked like.

'As someone who's met so many murderers . . .'

While others were very proud to shake hands with a man whose picture regularly appeared in the newspapers.

This did not apply to Bellamy. The doctor considered Maigret as an equal, in a way. He seemed to acknowledge that they were in the same league though not quite on the same level.

His curiosity was mixed with respect, and was almost a homage.

'Half past four, doctor,' said one of his partners.

'So it is . . . I hadn't forgotten . . .'

He seemed impervious to irony. He was probably aware of his reputation as a besotted husband and felt no shame. He made his way calmly over to the telephone booth. Maigret could see his sharp profile through the glass sides and felt a growing urge to talk to him.

How? It was almost as delicate as with the nuns. Wait until the doctor left, follow him to the door and say:

'May I walk a little way with you?'

Childish. Childish too, with a man like that, to request a medical consultation.

Maigret was part of the little group while remaining an outsider. People were used to seeing him sitting at his usual table. Occasionally, one of the bridge players would show him his hand. Or someone would ask him:

'You're not too bored here in Les Sables d'Olonne?'

But he still remained an onlooker. A bit like a day boy among the boarders at a school.

'Is your wife feeling better?'

As a matter of fact, had Doctor Bellamy ever spoken to him directly? He tried in vain to remember.

He was tired of this holiday which was throwing him off-balance, making him ridiculously shy. Even Mansuy, because this was his fiefdom, because later on he would be going back to his police station, had more composure than him.

Because a girl was dead, because a nun who was the picture of piety had slipped a note into his pocket, he was hanging around Doctor Bellamy the way a schoolboy hangs around the rich kid in the class.

'Waiter, another white wine.'

He didn't want to look at the doctor any more. His staring was becoming too obvious. The doctor must be able to tell what was going on in his mind, understand his reticence, and he was perhaps even laughing at it.

The doctor had finished his game. He rose and went to fetch his hat from the coat stand.

'Goodbye, gentlemen . . .'

He didn't say 'See you tomorrow', since the next day was the day of the funeral.

He was about to leave. He was walking past Maigret. No, he had paused for a moment.

'Were you about to leave, monsieur?'

He hadn't said 'inspector', but 'monsieur', perhaps with a hint of affectation.

'I was planning to, yes . . .'

'If you're going in the same direction as I am . . .'

It was strange. He was cordial, but his cordiality was cold, aloof.

For the first time in a long while, for the first time in his life perhaps, Maigret had the feeling that he wasn't the one calling the tune, but that he was being manipulated by the other person at will.

All the same, he followed. Chief Inspector Mansuy had witnessed the scene with a certain surprise.

Still calm, controlled, without irony, Bellamy held the door open for him. The beach spread out in front of them, with its thousands of children and mothers, and the pastel swimming hats of the bathers against the blue of the sea.

'You probably know where I live?'

'Your house was pointed out to me and I admired it.'

'Perhaps you'd like to see the interior?'

It was so direct, so unexpected, that Maigret was temporarily at a loss for words. Lighting a cigarette with a gold lighter – a gesture that showed off his beautiful, carefully manicured hands – the doctor said in a detached tone:

'I believe you are keen to get to know me?'

'I have heard a lot about you.'

'People have been talking about me a great deal in the last two days.'

Silence did not make him uncomfortable. He felt no need to talk for the sake of keeping the conversation going. His gait was sprightly. A few people greeted him, and he returned their greeting, doffing his hat in the same way to a market woman in a traditional lace headdress as for a dowager in an open-topped car driven by a liveried chauffeur.

'You would have come sooner or later, wouldn't you?'

That could mean a lot of things. Perhaps simply that eventually Maigret would have managed to get himself invited to the doctor's house.

'I hate wasting time, just as I hate ambiguous situations. Do you think that I killed my sister-in-law?'

This time, Maigret had to make a huge effort to keep pace with this man who, there in the sunshine, among the idle crowd of holidaymakers, was asking him such a brutal question.

He did not smile, did not protest. It took him only a few seconds to formulate his reply, which he gave in the same calm tone as that in which the question had been asked.

'Two nights ago,' he said, 'I didn't know yet that she was dead, or that she was your sister-in-law, but I had already begun to take an interest in her.'

3.

Had Maigret hoped to catch him off-guard? If he had, he was to be disappointed. First of all, Doctor Bellamy appeared not to have heard his words, which had been drowned out by the growing noise from the beach and the sea. He had the time to take a few steps before the echo of Maigret's statement, rather than his actual voice, reached him.

Then his expression betrayed a faint surprise. He gave his companion a little wink, as if trying to find a reason for this ambiguity. Meanwhile, faced with a partner who was a match for him, Maigret was so alert, so receptive, that he felt able to capture Doctor Bellamy's slightest nuance of thought, and he sensed a slight disappointment, a silent admonition.

A few seconds later, it was already over, Bellamy gave the matter no further thought and the two of them continued along the promenade, in step with one another. Both men automatically gazed at the elegant curve of the beach which had something feminine, almost sensual, about it. It was the hour when the sea began to grow paler, shimmering slightly, before the flaming sunset.

'You were born in the countryside, weren't you?' asked Bellamy.

Their thoughts, like their footsteps, were in tune again,

as if, like long-term lovers, they no longer needed to speak in lengthy sentences, but only a sort of linguistic short-hand.

'I was born in the countryside, yes.'

'I was born in an ancient house that my family owns a few kilometres from here, in the marshes.'

He hadn't said chateau, but Maigret knew that the Bellamy family owned a chateau in the region.

'Which province are you from?'

Others would have said 'department', and Maigret appreciated the use of the word province, which he liked.

'The Bourbonnais.'

This was not idle curiosity. There was nothing mundane about Bellamy's questions.

'Your parents were farmers?'

'My father was an estate manager in charge of around twenty smallholdings.'

Doctor Bellamy was asking him exactly the questions he would have asked, but he did not take offence, quite the opposite. They continued walking in silence. In silence too, they crossed the road, just beyond the casino. Doctor Bellamy automatically reached into his pocket for his key. He paused for a moment on the threshold, groped around and pushed open the white-painted door.

Maigret entered, showing no discomfiture or surprise. He stepped on to the thick carpet in the hall and immediately felt surrounded by comfort and well-being.

It would have been hard to design a calmer, more harmonious interior. It was lavish without being oppressive, with nothing to arrest the eye, and the light itself had a quality that could be savoured like a good wine, like certain sparkling spring mornings. The drawing rooms, whose armchairs looked as if they had been vacated only a few moments earlier, boasted huge bay windows.

A wide staircase with a wrought-iron banister led to the upper floors. The doctor started to make his way upstairs.

'If you would like to follow me into my study . . .'

He didn't take the trouble to conceal a certain smugness. There was a barely perceptible glint of pride in his eyes.

They went upstairs, without hurrying, and then a slight incident occurred. A door opened above their heads. For Maigret, it was just a door, since he was not familiar with the layout of the rooms, but the doctor had already recognized the sound of that particular door. He frowned. They heard footsteps on the stair carpet, beyond the first bend. They were light, faltering steps, the steps of someone who was no more familiar with the house than Maigret.

The person coming down must have heard them and leaned over the banister. They looked up, and saw a girl's small head. Their eyes met, only for a second, and there was panic in the eyes of the visitor who dithered, as if she was about to go back upstairs to avoid them.

Instead, she suddenly darted forwards and they saw all of her on the landing, a tall, skinny girl of around fourteen, whose legs were too spindly, wearing a slightly faded cotton frock. Why was Maigret particularly struck by a little coloured-bead bag which she clutched nervously?

She seemed to be calculating her move, assessing how much room she had to pass them, and then she made a dash for it. Keeping her face averted and staying close to the wall, she slipped past them, raced down the stairs and almost banged into the front door, groping frantically for the door knob, as in a nightmare when you are being pursued by danger and you run into a blank wall.

The doctor swung round at the same time as Maigret. The door opened, an oblong of brighter light appeared and swallowed up the girl.

That was all. It was nothing. Bellamy looked up again. Wondered whether someone was on the landing watching them. He was taken aback, vexed, anxious perhaps?

Maigret could sense that there was something unforeseen, something inexplicable about this encounter.

Bellamy resumed his ascent. Now they could see the door the girl had come out of, but it was shut. They walked past it, down a wide corridor, and Bellamy pushed open another door much further along.

'Come in, monsieur. Make yourself comfortable. It goes without saying that if you feel hot, you may remove your jacket.'

They were in a vast study lined with books. As they entered, they were dazzled by the sun pouring in through the three big bay windows. Bellamy, with a movement that must have been habitual, lowered the venetian blinds and the light softened and was transformed into a golden dust.

Above the fireplace was a magnificent portrait of a woman, an oil painting, and there was a photograph of the same woman in a silver frame on the desk.

The doctor picked up the intercom and waited for a few moments.

'Is that you, Mother? You don't need me?'

A piercing voice came out of the receiver, and because it was so loud, the speech was garbled and Maigret was unable to catch a single word.

'I'm busy at the moment, yes. Would you send Francis to me?'

They were silent until the arrival of the butler in a white linen jacket.

'I shan't ask you if you'd like a whisky . . . Or a port either, no doubt? . . . Would you like a glass of dry Pouilly? . . . A bottle of Pouilly, Francis . . . The usual for me . . .'

He glanced quickly at some envelopes lying on his desk, without opening them.

'Would you excuse me for a moment?'

He left the room on the heels of the butler. Was it to ask him about the girl they had met on the stairs? Was he going into the room on the landing and would he, on his return, call the woman in the photograph and the portrait?

Chief Inspector Mansuy had not been exaggerating. Even among the crowds in the street, it would have been impossible not to notice her. And yet the most striking thing about her was an extraordinary simplicity. Her demeanour was calm, modest. She seemed shy, scared of people staring at her. Her initial instinct must be fear of everything that was new or unfamiliar.

She had big, light-blue, almost violet eyes and a childlike face, and yet she was very much a woman, and you could imagine a curvaceous figure, and soft, fragrant flesh.

'Forgive me for leaving you alone . . .'

Bellamy, who had caught his guest contemplating the

photograph, pretended not to notice. However, opening a drawer, he said:

'Her sister was very different, as you will see.'

He riffled through some photographs and held one out to Maigret. And it was indeed a completely different face, a young brunette with an elongated face and irregular features. She wore a high-necked dress, without jewellery, which gave her a sober, austere look.

'They're not at all alike, are they? You have probably already been told that they are not from the same father and it is very possible, it is likely . . . Admit, monsieur, that you would have come to see me sooner or later . . . I don't know what pretext you would have found . . . For my part, I confess that, these events notwithstanding, I wanted to have a chat with you . . .'

It was curious: his cordiality was so natural, so unaffected, that it was arid. He never took the trouble to smile. The rattle of glasses could be heard on the other side of the door, and Francis brought in a tray with a misted bottle, whisky, ice and glasses.

'I shan't tell you that you may smoke your pipe. That goes without saying. Perhaps I should have waited until the funeral to invite you. It takes place tomorrow, as you know. As you also know, the body isn't in the house.'

He took his watch out of his pocket, and Maigret understood. It was around this time that the autopsy was due to take place.

'I was very fond of my sister-in-law. Or rather, I considered her to be my own sister. When she came to this house, she was thirteen and had plaits down her back.'

Maigret was reminded of the girl they had met on the stairs, and Bellamy, who guessed his thoughts, frowned slightly, displaying the tiniest hint of impatience.

'Forgive me for not drinking the same as you. To your good health! . . . Lili was a highly strung child, inquisitive, a little wild, and crazy about music. If you are interested, later on I'll show you what we called – what she herself called – her sanctuary.'

He drank the whisky slowly, set down his glass and went and sat at the desk, which in no way resembled a work desk, and indicated an armchair where Maigret should sit.

He did not allow Maigret the chance to take the initiative, which neither vexed Maigret nor made him feel humiliated. A fly on the wall would have found him awkward, self-conscious. His gaze was dull, his movements heavy, while the doctor, on the other hand, was not taken in.

'You are on holiday, so I've been told. I've seen you a few times watching our games of bridge, which have become a vital need for most of us. As far as I'm concerned, it's practically the only moment in the day that I spend outside this house, and I consider this habit as necessary for my health. Which reminds me, forgive me for not inquiring after your wife. She is in the hands of our best surgeon. Bertrand is a friend of mine.'

He hadn't been insincere when he'd said that he had been taking an interest in Maigret from the start.

'You have also become acquainted with the atmosphere of our hospital and with our nuns.'

The ghost of a smile. He was picturing a clumsy Maigret among the nuns with their muffled tread.

There was a tricky obstacle to overcome. He still had to explain this spontaneous invitation, his anxiety to dispel any prejudices that this detective chief inspector might have been harbouring against him.

Did he suspect the note from Sister Marie des Anges?

'You have probably spent time in a little town like ours before. Mind you, I love the place and won't speak ill of it. If I am here, it is because I wanted to be . . .'

He gazed around affectionately at the surroundings he had created for himself. When his gaze rested on the venetian blinds letting in streaks of light, Maigret guessed that he was thinking of the sea with its sails and its seagulls, which he could see from his study in the morning, while he savoured the quality of the air and the subtlest fragrances from the moment he opened his eyes.

'I love the peace and quiet . . . I love my house . . .'

As he also loved his books with their beautiful bindings, the curios dotted around the room that awaited the caress of his fingers.

'I could quite easily have become antisocial, and perhaps that is why I force myself to play bridge every day. It sounds straightforward and natural, doesn't it? Each person's life sounds straightforward until an event occurs and then people scrutinize us, no longer as ourselves, but in relation to that event. I think that is why I invited you to come. I didn't think twice about it at the time. I saw you looking at me several times. May I ask you a personal question? What was your training?'

It was Maigret's turn to appear more docile than the most docile of his 'customers'.

'I dreamed of being a doctor and I did my first three years of medicine. My father's death put an end to my studies and I joined the police by chance.'

He was not afraid that Bellamy would be shocked by the word in this refined, bourgeois atmosphere.

'I was going to say to you,' replied Bellamy, 'that your eyes always seem to be searching for a diagnosis. For the last two days, a lot of people have been staring at me with curiosity, some with involuntary alarm. Oh yes! I can feel it. I don't think I am liked, because I am not bothered about endearing myself to people. Did you know that that is generally what people are the least willing to forgive their fellow human beings? That is probably why so few men have the courage to live their lives without worrying what people think of them.

'I wasn't worried, two days ago. And I'm still not worried now. But I did feel the need to explain myself to you . . .'

As if he were afraid of having betrayed a certain vulnerability or a weakness, he added hastily, with a faint smile that Maigret was beginning to recognize:

'Perhaps I was simply trying to avoid complications? I realized that you were intrigued, that you wanted to know, that you would try to find out at all costs. Some men put off irksome things until later and others deal with them straight away. I am one of the latter.'

'And I am a very irksome "thing", aren't I?'

'Not terribly. You don't know me. You don't know the

town. Anything that people tell you is likely to be twisted and you don't like that, admit it, you are only happy when you *feel* the truth in your bones.'

He seized the portrait of his sister-in-law and looked at it.

'I was very fond of that girl, but I repeat that my feelings for her were purely fraternal. I am aware that things are often otherwise. A man can easily be in love with two sisters, especially if they are both living under his roof. That is not the case and, besides, Lili was not in love with me. I'll go further. I was exactly the opposite of what she loved. She found me cold and cynical. She often said that I had no heart.

'All this of course is no proof that the accident was indeed an accident, but . . .'

Maigret listened to him while continuing to think about the girl on the stairs. There was no doubt that Doctor Bellamy had been shocked by her presence in the house. Initially, he had been taken aback. He had looked at her as if she were a stranger and was visibly wondering what she was doing in his home.

Afterwards, when all of her had appeared on the landing, he had known who she was, Maigret had read it in his eyes.

He probably knew at that moment whom she had come to see.

The household was no doubt unaccustomed to seeing new faces. Hadn't Chief Inspector Mansuy spoken of the jealousy of the doctor who, when he went out, even simply to play bridge, left his wife under the supervision of his mother?

But someone had come. And immediately Bellamy had telephoned the elderly lady. If the girl had been visiting her, presumably she would have told him straight away, although her son would have avoided asking her about it in front of Maigret.

As far as Maigret could tell, she hadn't mentioned the matter. And then Bellamy had left the room and headed towards the door on the landing.

What had the doctor just said?

'All this of course is no proof that the accident was indeed an accident, but . . .'

And Maigret replied, almost without thinking:

'I'm sure you never had any intention of killing your sister-in-law . . .'

If the nuance did not escape the doctor, he refrained from commenting on it.

'Others are, and will be, less positive than you. For my part, I wanted to open the door of this house to you. It will remain open to you. I hope that you'll see that there are no secrets here. Would you like to have a look around my sister-in-law's apartment? You'll be able to meet my mother, who must be up there right now.'

He drained his glass and gave the visitor time to finish his. Then he opened a door and they walked through a second, more private, library where there was a green divan. Another door and, still facing the sea, they entered a very soberly decorated room, verging on the austere, where most of the space was taken up by a grand piano. On the walls were photographs of composers. Few armchairs, almost no fabrics, a plain carpet.

'This was her realm,' said the doctor, walking towards a half-open door.

He added, speaking to someone who was invisible:

'Mother, I'd like to introduce the famous Chief Inspector Maigret to you.'

A sort of groan came from the adjacent room; a tiny, very fat woman dressed in black from head to toe appeared, leaning on a walking stick with an ivory knob. Her expression was wary, not particularly affable. She looked the intruder up and down and merely said:

'Monsieur . . .'

'I apologize for disturbing you today, madame, but your son insisted that I accompany him home.'

She glowered at the doctor, who explained with his faint smile:

'Monsieur Maigret is on holiday at Les Sables d'Olonne. He is someone I have always wanted to meet and, since he'll be leaving us sooner or later, I was afraid of missing him. We were talking about Lili and I was keen to show him what we call her sanctuary.'

'It's very untidy,' she grumbled.

All the same, she allowed them in and Maigret found himself in a bedroom that was almost as bare, almost as unfeminine as the music room, despite the clothes that had been taken out of a wardrobe and were heaped on the bed. Among other things, there was a black velvet toque with no trimmings, without a splash of colour, that must have been part of a sort of uniform for the girl.

There was not a single photograph on the walls, or on the furniture, nothing that suggested family life.

'These are the surroundings she loved. She had no friends, male or female. Once a week she would spend a day in Nantes where she would have a lesson with her teacher. When there was an interesting concert in the region, I would drive her to it. Let us go down this way . . .'

Maigret bowed to the elderly lady and followed his host down a spiral staircase. They were back on the ground floor, in a sort of glass conservatory that opened on to a very well-maintained garden where a few magnificent trees provided shade. To the right, a vast, airy kitchen could be glimpsed.

'Do you sometimes regret having gone into the police?'

'No.'

'I thought not. I wondered several times when I was looking at you.'

They walked through the drawing rooms and Doctor Bellamy opened the front door.

'I have noticed, in any case, that you haven't asked me a single question.'

'What would be the point?'

And Maigret re-lit his pipe, which he had put out with his thumb on entering the girl's apartment.

As he took leave of his guest, Bellamy was a little ill at ease. Had this visit disappointed him? Did Maigret's silence now make him somewhat anxious?

Not once had the doctor mentioned his wife and there had been no question of introducing her to Maigret.

'I hope, monsieur, that I shall have the pleasure of seeing you again.'

'So do I,' muttered Maigret as he walked off.

Maigret was almost pleased with himself. He puffed on his pipe as he made his way towards the town centre. Then he looked at the time and retraced his steps, picking up his walk where he should have been at that hour, passing familiar landmarks: the port, the billowing sails, the smell of tarmac and heating oil, the boats gliding down the channel and mooring in front of the fish market.

Only he turned around to look at every girl he passed and stared into every open doorway, in the hope of catching sight of the girl from the staircase.

She had not been wearing the local costume of short, black-silk skirts like most of the fishermen's daughters or the women who worked in the sardine canneries. And yet she was of a very humble background. Her dress had been faded, her black woollen stockings darned and her little coloured-bead bag came from a bazaar or local fair.

Behind the port there was a warren of narrow streets which Maigret explored every day. The houses were only one storey high, sometimes there was just a ground floor. Generally, and this was something he had only seen in Les Sables d'Olonne, the cellar served as the kitchen, with stone steps leading up to the street.

It was highly likely that the girl lived in this neighbourhood.

He went into his fishermen's café and drank a glass of white wine. Once the door had closed, Doctor Bellamy must have raced upstairs to join his wife or his mother. Which of the two had he questioned about the girl's visit?

Maigret walked, as he did every day, but without realizing it he took a detour and found himself outside the police station. It wasn't far from the railway station. A train must just have arrived, because there were people walking past carrying suitcases.

A couple caught his attention, or rather he stood there in amazement on seeing a woman who so closely resembled the two portraits in the doctor's study that it was uncanny.

This woman was no longer young. She must have been getting on for fifty and yet she had the same hair of an ethereal blonde, the same violet eyes. She was only slightly plumper, while still preserving an extraordinary lightness.

The woman wore a white suit and a white hat, which made her stand out among the shabby crowd in the street. Leaving a trail of perfume in her wake, she walked quite fast, dragging along a man around fifteen years her senior who did not look at ease.

In her hand, she held a very expensive crocodile-skin attaché-case, while her companion struggled with two suitcases.

She could be no other than Madame Godreau, the mother of Odette Bellamy and of Lili.

They must have sent a telegram to Paris, and she had hastened here for the funeral.

Maigret gazed after the pair. There were several hotels nearby, but they did not go into any of them. Were they going to ring the bell of the house that Maigret had just left?

He entered the police station and slowly climbed the dusty staircase. He had only been here once and he already felt at home. Without knocking, he pushed open the door of the inspectors' office, which was almost deserted, as it had been the previous day. It was past six o'clock. Chief Inspector Mansuy was busy signing letters.

'Madame Godreau has arrived,' announced Maigret, perching on the corner of the desk.

'Ah! . . . For the funeral, of course . . . But how do you know?'

'I just saw her leaving the station.'

'Do you know her?'

'You only need to have seen a picture of her daughter to recognize her.'

'I've never met her. Apparently, she's still beautiful . . .'

'Very . . . and she knows it . . .'

A few more flourishes.

'Have you had an interesting afternoon?'

'Doctor Bellamy talked a great deal and did me the honour of showing me around his home. Tell me, do you by any chance know a girl of around fourteen or fifteen, tall and skinny, with reddish hair who wears a pink cotton dress and black woollen stockings?'

The inspector looked at him in surprise.

'Is that all you know about her?'

'She has a little handbag made of coloured beads.'

'And you don't know where she lives?'

'No.'

'You don't know her name?'

'Neither her first name nor her surname.'

'Nor do you know where she works?'

'I don't even know if she has a job.'

'You do realize that Les Sables d'Olonne has twenty

thousand souls and that the streets are crawling with girls like the one you have just described?'

'But I want to find this particular one.'

'In which neighbourhood did you meet her?'

'At Doctor Bellamy's.'

'And you didn't ask him . . . I'm sorry! I understand . . . That's already a clue, of course . . .'

Maigret smiled, and slowly filled a fresh pipe.

'Look. I feel as though I'm bothering you. I'm here on holiday, that's a fact. What is happening at Les Sables d'Olonne is none of my business. And yet I'd give a lot to find that girl.'

'I can try.'

'I don't know whether she'll return to the doctor's house. To be honest, I don't think so. But who knows whether she might go and hang around the house? It's highly likely that tomorrow she'll be standing along the route of the funeral procession. Maybe if you have a word with one of your men . . .'

Mansuy was beginning to worry.

'Do you think he killed his sister-in-law? The coroner's just telephoned me—'

'And his report is negative, I'm sure.'

'Correct. You've heard? Her head hit the road. Her body somersaulted a couple of times. It curled into a ball like a hare when it's shot. But all the injuries are consistent with the tears and stains on her clothes. She could have been pushed, of course, but without being hit, without her defending herself . . .'

'She wasn't pushed.'

'So you believe it was an accident?'

'I don't know.'

'You've just said that she wasn't pushed . . .'

'I know nothing,' sighed Maigret who had become more solemn. 'The fact is, I know no more than you do. Perhaps less, because I don't know Les Sables d'Olonne. All the same, I'd like to find that girl. I'd also like to have a private talk with Sister Marie des Anges, which is even harder. Have you ever called a nun in for questioning?'

'No,' replied the stocky inspector, flabbergasted.

'Me neither. I can only hope that she'll write to me again.'

He was talking to himself, without taking the trouble to enlighten his colleague.

'Come and have a drink . . . By the way, your Polyte yesterday, did he confess?'

'He won't confess. He's never confessed in his life. This is at least the tenth time we've caught him red-handed and each time he hotly denies it.'

They stopped at a café full of regulars and, all the way there, Maigret had continued to look about him on the off chance he might spot the girl.

'You see, Mansuy, there is something we don't know, something that's not right, and I have a hunch that if we can track down this girl . . .'

He ordered an aperitif instead of his usual white wine. Then, as Mansuy insisted on buying a round, he downed another, on top of all the white wines he'd drunk during the day. There was smoke all round him and the haze of alcohol was so thick that it billowed out several metres on to the pavement.

'Look, Mansuy . . .'

He seized his colleague's arm.

'I think it's more important than it seems to find this girl . . . It's none of my business, I repeat . . . It's not so much as a professional that I'm speaking . . .'

'If you want us to go back to the police station, I'll write a memo this evening.'

'Do you know whether the doctor's butler is married, whether he sleeps in the house?'

Poor Mansuy had never imagined that an inspector from the Police Judiciaire could carry out an investigation in such a manner.

'I'll find out . . . I confess I'd never worried about . . .'

Maigret was talking to himself:

'It would be the way to find out . . .'

Then to Mansuy:

'Let's go back to your office, yes . . . Don't hold it against me . . . I can't explain. . . I am so certain that it would be better . . .'

They entered the secretary's office on the ground floor, where there was a coffee tin on a little spirit stove.

'Tell me, Dubois, do you know Doctor Bellamy's butler, by any chance?'

'Isn't he a fairly young, blond fellow?'

It was Maigret who replied.

'Yes, his name is Francis . . .'

'He's Belgian,' stated the secretary. 'I remember because he came two or three times to get his residence permit stamped . . .'

'Married?'

'Wait . . . He's on my list . . . I'll find him . . .'

It wasn't as straightforward as all that. The list was nowhere to be found. The day secretary had left with the key to some drawers. Eventually they found it where it should not have been.

'Here we are . . . Francis-Charles-Albert Decoin, born in Huy . . . age thirty-two . . . Married to Laurence Van Offel, cook . . . She had her permit stamped too . . . Hold on . . . Hôtel du Remblai . . . No, she left . . . Her most recent address was the Hôtel Bellevue, where she was working as a kitchen girl as recently as two months ago . . .'

Mansuy was still looking at Maigret inquisitively. As they left the police station, he asked him timidly:

'Are you really . . .'

He did not finish. He gave a sweeping gesture that took in the town, the hotels. Was it possible that his distinguished colleague intended to go from one improbable address to another, questioning porters and chambermaids like a rookie inspector?

'With your permission, I'll instruct one of my men . . .'

Was the man serious? Just as Maigret felt he had both feet on the ground? Why not bring in Sister Marie des Anges and Doctor Bellamy too?

Maigret finally had something concrete to do.

Something that was perhaps of no use, no importance . . .

He thrust his hands in his pockets as if it were the depths of winter, while his teeth clenched the stem of his pipe a little harder.

'You'll keep me informed? . . . Should I look for this girl anyway? . . .'

Maigret forgot to answer and shook Mansuy's hand as they parted company on a street corner, then headed for the imposing building of the Hôtel Bellevue, the most luxurious establishment on Le Remblai.

A kitchen girl, at least that would make a change from nuns and neurologists.

'Excuse me, porter . . . I'd like to speak to Laurence Decoin who works in the kitchens . . .'

'You'll have to go to the service entrance . . . Turn left . . . You'll find an alleyway . . . There's a door with frosted-glass panes and a goods lift . . . It's there . . .'

A few moments later, Maigret, who hadn't found anyone to let him in, went up a staircase stinking of urine behind the scenes of the hotel, which reminded him of backstage in a little provincial theatre. He stopped a giant of a butcher between two swing doors through which waiters were dashing, and the latter looked at him with contempt:

'What is it?'

'I'd like to speak to Laurence Decoin.'

Then the butcher became almost fierce.

'And what else . . . Who's asking for her, if you please, "young man"?'

'A friend . . .'

'Really? . . . Laurence! . . .' he yelled. 'Come here and let me introduce a friend. . . A friend of yours, so he says . . .'

A chubby blonde came towards them, wiping her hands on her apron, and it was clear that the doctor's young butler was no longer of much importance in her life and that in any case she was scared to death of the hairy butcher.

'I don't know who this man is, do you, Fernand?' she exclaimed in a strong accent.

'Well, what do you have to say for yourself, eh?'

He advanced, as solid and menacing as a tank.

Maigret felt himself come alive again.

4.

'I apologize,' he said with the utmost courtesy. 'It is true that I do not know Madame, and that I have never seen her. I simply want to ask her where I can meet her husband outside his employers' house.'

She turned first of all towards Fernand, triumphantly:

'You see, you silly, jealous boy, it's not what you thought . . .'

Then to Maigret:

'Now what has Francis done?'

There was a door near them. It opened into a long, narrow, dingily lit room with the fanlight placed too high, where the electric lights burned all day. A table with two benches filled the entire length of the room, like an army mess. It was the staff dining room where, at that moment, there were only two waiters sitting at the far end, eating in silence. This was the room that Laurence showed him into, so as not to get under the feet of the bustling waiters.

'You're from the police, aren't you? That doesn't worry me, mind you. It would even be a good thing if he were in big trouble because that would help me get a divorce, wouldn't it, Fernand?'

She was sturdy and on the short side, with a slightly snub nose, but there was something fresh about her.

'When I think that I'm the one who has to pay for the

kid's upkeep with what I earn here, because that loafer doesn't want to know—'

'You don't live with him?'

It was Fernand who answered, in order to dot the 'i's once and for all:

'We've been together for two years now.'

'Do you happen to know whether he has a room in town?'

The plump Laurence burst out laughing:

'A room and all the rest too, you mean! And his slippers by the bed . . .'

She suddenly grew suspicious:

'You're not from the local police?'

'I am from Paris.'

'Because anyone from around here would know that Francis knocks about with La Popine—'

'La Popine?'

'Madame Popineau. . . The fishmonger . . . The one who has a pretty shop on the corner of Rue de la République . . . A tough bitch, you don't want to mess with her . . . People say she's already worn out three husbands, even though they were strapping fellows. She's kept busy visiting their graves on All Saints' Day . . . It won't be long before poor Francis . . . I even wonder how the poor thing manages to satisfy her . . . In any case, you're almost bound to find him at her place after ten o'clock at night . . . Tell me, monsieur, is it serious?'

Maigret avoided replying in order to learn more.

'He can't help it . . . He can't stop himself nicking little things . . . It's not even to sell them, mind you . . . It's to give them to women . . . Because he always needs to impress them . . .'

She burst out laughing, giving Fernand a knowing look:

'You impress them with what you can, isn't that right, monsieur?'

Maigret dined in a corner, all alone, and he wasn't wearing exactly the expression they were familiar with at the Hôtel Bel Air. Monsieur Léonard waited for him in vain for their nightly chat in the back room. Once Maigret had finished eating, he went for a walk in the dark. The sky was studded with light from the gas lamps and the waves were phosphorescent.

It was still too early, barely nine thirty. He walked past the doctor's house and saw that the lights were on. Then he came to the port, the little cafés where you have to go inside to sit down for a moment. He would have found it hard to say what was going on in his mind. His thoughts were vague, slightly disjointed. They began with Sister Marie des Anges. The calm convent atmosphere that was rubbing off on Madame Maigret herself.

Then the doctor and his beautiful, genteel house, his calm way of speaking and his piercing eyes.

Then, suddenly, a flaxen-haired girl sent him to the sordid underbelly of the Hôtel Bellevue, and there was Fernand the butcher, and the plump Laurence with her raucous laugh.

There were few passers-by in the narrow streets, where there was the occasional yellowish oblong of a shop and most of the windows were open. People went to bed early.

From the street you could almost imagine them, tossing and turning in beds damp with sweat. Sometimes, passing a dark window, he heard whisperings, so close that he felt as if he were intruding on someone's privacy and was tempted to walk on tiptoe, like at the hospital.

He asked for Madame Popineau's house. It stood at the end of the dock, in the new part of town, a fine house built of pretty pink bricks. The shop's shutters were closed. It had its own front door, in varnished oak, with a brass letterbox and door knob. He bent over and peeked through the keyhole like when he was a child, and saw a light inside.

It was eleven o'clock. When he rang the bell he heard the sound of a chair being scraped back, voices, footsteps. The door opened into a corridor that smelled of linoleum, with a bamboo coat stand to the right, and house plants in earthenware plant-pot holders.

'Forgive me, madame . . .'

In front of him stood a woman of around the same build as the plump Laurence, short and fat too, but a brunette, wearing the local costume, with a pretty starched head-dress that lit up her face.

'What is it?' she asked, trying to fathom out his features in the dark.

'I'd like to have a few words with Francis.'

'Come in.'

The door on the left was ajar. It opened into a dining room that looked brand new, with its red and yellow linoleum, brass plant-pot holders, knick-knacks and carved oak Henry II-style furniture.

Doctor Bellamy's butler was there, in felt slippers,

wearing no jacket or waistcoat, his open shirt revealing his chest. Ensconced deep in an armchair, his legs crossed, a small glass within reach, a pipe in his mouth, he was quietly reading the newspaper.

There was another armchair facing him, that of La Popine, with another small glass and an illustrated weekly.

'It's Monsieur Maigret who wants to talk to you, Francis . . .'

The Belgian was less surprised than Maigret himself.

'You know me?' asked Maigret.

'Don't think that I don't see you walk past every day! . . . I recognized you at once, at least a week ago . . . I said to Babette, I did: "That, my love, is the famous Detective Chief Inspector Maigret, or I'm not La Popine . . ."'

'I think I've still got somewhere an illustrated magazine from three weeks ago which has an article about you in it, with a lovely photo . . .'

Francis had risen to his feet, embarrassed. It was as if, without his livery, he felt naked in front of Maigret.

'Don't be afraid, silly! . . . I'm sure he's not here about you but about your boss . . . Am I in the way, inspector? . . . Because I can always go into my bedroom . . . Except that if it's information you want, I can probably give you more than Francis . . . Sit down . . . You'll have a little drink with us, won't you? . . . I have to tell you that I've always loved crime stories, so I've known about you for at least fifteen years . . . When I see a juicy murder, nice and complicated, I say: "I hope it's Maigret who's handling it . . ."'

'And in the morning I open my newspaper before putting the water for the coffee on to boil . . .'

Maigret sat down. He had no option. And it was cosy, almost family-like. The fishmonger must be proud of her furniture, her gleaming copper pots, her trinkets, proud of this interior that was so typically petty bourgeois.

When all was said and done, were her dreams so different from Madame Maigret's?

Francis was less at ease and wanted to put on his jacket. It was the woman who stopped him.

'No need to feel awkward in front of the inspector! If everything that's written about him is true, he doesn't mind you being in your shirt-sleeves, quite the opposite. He's the one who's going to make himself comfortable . . .'

A door to the left opened into the shop, all in marble, which exuded a faint smell of fish.

'Do *you* think it was an accident, Monsieur Maigret?'

It was clearly one of those days. At Doctor Bellamy's already, he had been the one who had been interrogated.

'Mind you, I don't want to speak ill of that man . . . I knew him as a boy . . . I think I'm three or four years older than he is, and I'm not ashamed to say so . . .'

Even though she was in her fifties, she was astonishingly youthful, truly delectable still. She had filled Maigret's glass and held hers out to clink glasses.

'I knew his father too . . . He was the same type of man. Not talkative . . . and yet you can't say that they're proud . . . I mean, they're gentlemen, but they don't shove it in your face all the time. But the mother, now she's something else . . . That woman, Monsieur Maigret, let La Popine tell you, she's a nasty piece of work . . . And, if something bad happened, I'm absolutely certain that it was her fault . . . Do you think the doctor will be arrested?'

'It is out of the question.'

This was awkward. He was not in charge of any investigation. He wanted a simple piece of information. And the next day, thanks to La Popine, the whole town would know that Chief Inspector Maigret was going around asking questions about Doctor Bellamy.

This could go far, and turn into an unpleasant business, and yet Maigret couldn't bring himself to regret being there. He puffed gently on his pipe, warmed the glass in his hands and averted his eyes from the fat woman who sat with her legs splayed, revealing large expanses of pink thigh above her black stockings.

He finally managed to get a word in.

'I wanted to ask Francis a question . . .'

'How did you know I was here?'

Maigret was about to give some vague answer, but La Popine didn't give him the time.

'If you think, my boy, that the whole world doesn't know . . . Mind you, Monsieur Maigret, I want to marry him, I do . . . He wouldn't be the first . . . Unfortunately, there's already a wife, and she won't hear of a divorce . . .'

'Tell me, Francis . . . This afternoon, when I went to Doctor Bellamy's, a girl came out of an upstairs bedroom. I presume it was you who opened the door to her?'

'It's always me who opens the door,' he said.

'So you saw her. Do you know who she is?'

'I was wondering the same thing myself.'

'You don't know her?'

'No. She's been to the house twice. The first time was on the 2nd of August, when Madame was so ill . . .'

'One moment, Francis, if you don't mind.'

'Yes, take your time, darling . . . Let the inspector speak . . .'

'The accident of which Mademoiselle Godreau was a victim took place on the 3rd of August . . . Is that right?'

'That's correct . . . The day of the concert—'

'And on the 2nd of August, Madame Bellamy was very ill, you say?'

'That's correct . . . And even on the 1st of August . . . On the 1st of August she didn't get out of bed . . .'

'Is she often ill?'

'I've never known her to stay in bed all day . . .'

'Did they call for a doctor?'

'It was Monsieur who attended her . . . He's a doctor . . .'

'Of course . . .'

Except that a doctor has no hesitation in calling on a fellow doctor to attend his family, particularly if he is a specialist.

'You don't know what was wrong with her?'

'No . . .'

'Did you go into her room?'

'Never! . . . Even when she's not there, it's forbidden . . . Doctor Bellamy will not allow any man to set foot in Madame's bedroom . . . Once, when there was no one in the house and Jeanne, the maid, was in the apartment, I went in . . . I took one or two steps, because I needed to speak to Jeanne—'

'And are we meant to believe that all you did was talk to her?'

'The doctor arrived without making a sound . . . He's never been so sharp with me . . . At one point I thought he was going to hit me.'

'So,' repeated Maigret, 'on the 1st of August, two days before her sister's death, Odette Bellamy was ill and didn't get out of bed . . . And that was when, you say, the girl came to see her for the first time?'

'Not the 1st of August, the 2nd—'

'You let her in . . . What time was it?'

'Around half past four . . .'

'In other words, the hour when the doctor plays cards at the Brasserie du Remblai . . . He can be seen from the pavement if a person wants to be certain that he's not at home . . .'

'Probably . . .'

'What did the girl say to you?'

'She asked to see Madame Bellamy . . . At first I thought she meant the doctor's mother . . .'

'Where was she at that moment?'

'In the laundry . . . It was the day the seamstress comes . . .'

'Let me explain,' said the fishmonger. 'She all but makes her own clothes, to save money. She's as stingy as a miser. She has an old humpbacked seamstress who togs her up any old how, but she doesn't care, as long as it doesn't cost much . . . I can tell you some stories . . . Listen! . . . When she telephoned me to ask for fish that wasn't so fresh for the servants' meals . . .'

'Just a moment, if you don't mind?'

'I'm sorry . . . Carry on!'

'You showed the girl upstairs?'

'No! . . . I told her that Madame was not at home . . . She asked me to go and inform her that it was little Lucile and that she had something very important to tell her . . .'

'So you went into the bedroom to deliver your message . . .'

'Excuse me! . . . I called Jeanne . . . I was certain that Madame would refuse to see the girl . . . But not at all, she asked for her to be shown up—'

'Did she stay long?'

'I don't know . . . I went back to the scullery, where I had to clean the silver . . .'

'Do you know, Monsieur Maigret, that it's Francis who polishes my copper pans? . . . even though my cleaning woman comes every day, he claims that women don't know how to scour—'

'When the girl came back today, did you take her straight upstairs?'

'I didn't need to announce her . . . I saw Jeanne on the landing, and she said: "Show her up, Francis . . ."'

'In other words, this time your employer was expecting Lucile?'

'I presume so . . .'

'Do you ever listen at the keyhole?'

'No, monsieur.'

'Why not?'

'Because of Doctor Bellamy's mother . . . She looks heavy, almost helpless . . . She leans on her stick as if she couldn't stand on her own two legs but she swoops down on you out of the blue . . . She's always roaming around the house . . .'

'A pest! . . . And to top it all, Monsieur Maigret, she isn't even from a good family . . . When she comes to the market with the cook, she yells at us as if we were trollops . . . She's forgotten that her father was a drunkard who they used to have to rescue from the gutter and that her mother was a charwoman . . . It's true that she was a beautiful girl . . . You wouldn't believe it to look at her now . . .'

'Tell me, Madame Popineau—'

'You can call me Popine, like everyone else!'

'Tell me, Popine – you know everyone at Les Sables d'Olonne – would you have any idea whose daughter this Lucile is?'

'Ten years ago, I'd have answered yes . . . I was still a "pedlar" . . . I went from door to door with my barrow selling fish . . . So you see, I knew all the urchins—'

'She's lanky and thin with hair that is almost colourless, straw-coloured . . .'

'Does she wear plaits?'

'No . . .'

'It's a pity because I know one but she wears plaits . . . She's the cooper's daughter . . .'

'Is she around fourteen or fifteen?'

'Probably older . . . She's already developed . . . A fine little bust—'

'Think hard . . .'

'I don't see . . . Mind you, just give me until tomorrow lunchtime . . . With all the people that come to my shop, it won't take me long to find out . . . The town isn't so big, after all . . .'

Maigret was to remember those words a little later. *The town isn't so big!*

'Francis, do you have the impression that your employers get on well?'

The Belgian was at a loss for an answer.

'Do they fight often?'

'Never.'

He was nonplussed at the thought that anyone could argue with the doctor.

'Does he sometimes speak to his wife sharply?'

'No, monsieur . . .'

Maigret realized that he would have to press the matter.

'Are they cheerful when they are together, at the table, for example? I presume you're the one who serves their meals?'

'Yes, monsieur.'

'Do they talk to each other much?'

'Monsieur talks . . . So does his mother . . .'

'Do you have the impression that Madame Bellamy is happy?'

'Sometimes, monsieur . . . It's hard to say . . . If you knew Monsieur better . . .'

'Try and explain what you mean.'

'I can't . . . He's not a man you talk to like anyone else . . . He looks at you and you feel all small—'

'Does his wife feel all small in front of him?'

'Maybe, sometimes . . . She sometimes talks like everyone else . . . She starts telling a story, laughing . . . Then she looks at him and stops in mid-sentence—'

'I think it's rather when she looks at her mother-in-law,' broke in La Popine. 'You have to understand, Monsieur Maigret, that a young woman like Odette – I knew her as a little girl too, and she wasn't stuck-up in those days – I say that a young woman like her isn't made to live with a witch . . . and old Madame Bellamy is just like a witch . . . It's not a walking stick but a broomstick she should have between her legs . . .'

Maigret briefly thought of the interrogation that the gentle Mansuy had conducted in front of him, when he was questioning Polyte. The latter had stubbornly clammed up, opening his mouth when forced to only to deny all evidence.

In contrast, these two talked nonstop, and yet it was just as difficult to get close to the truth.

He sensed that it was within reach. He had a whiff of it, trying in his mind to put each of them in their place around the family dinner table, for example, but there was always a detail that was wrong, that *rang false*.

It is not easy to see people through the eyes of a butler, of Madame Popineau's lover.

'Before being ill, how did Madame Bellamy spend her days?'

Poor Francis! La Popine encouraged him to talk, almost prompting him, like at school. He wanted to be helpful and tried to express himself as clearly as possible.

'I don't know . . . First of all, she would stay in her room till late morning and have her breakfast brought up to her.'

'At what time?'

'Around ten o'clock.'

'Just a moment . . . Do the doctor and his wife sleep in separate rooms?'

'Well, there are two bedrooms and two bathrooms, but I've never known Monsieur to sleep in his room.'

'Even these last two days?'

'I'm sorry! . . . Since the 3rd of August, he has slept alone . . . In the daytime, Madame often used to go into Mademoiselle's music room . . . She would sit in a corner and read, listening to the music—'

'Does she read a lot?'

'Whenever I see her she's nearly always got a book in her hand.'

'Does she go out?'

'Rarely without Monsieur . . . Or without her mother-in-law—'

'She never goes out alone?'

'She has done.'

'More often recently than before?'

'I don't know . . . It's a big house, you see . . . In the scullery there's a little notice board . . . It's Monsieur's mother who put it there . . . We are three servants, the cook, Jeanne and myself . . . On the notice board, we find our timetable for the whole day . . . At such-and-such a time we must be in such-and-such a room, doing such-and-such a job, and all hell breaks loose if we are found elsewhere . . .'

'Did the two sisters get on well?'

'I think so, yes . . .'

'At the table, was Lili more cheerful, or more talkative, than Odette?'

'It's six of one and half a dozen of the other . . .'

'I'm going to repeat my earlier question and I urge you to think hard: are you sure that it was the 1st of August, two days before her sister died, that your employer fell ill?'

'I'm certain.'

'Where does the doctor see his patients?'

'He doesn't see them in the house but in the annexe at the bottom of the garden. The annexe has a direct entrance from a little sidestreet—'

'Who opens the door to the patients?'

'No one. They ring the bell and the door opens automatically. The patients go into a waiting room. There are very few, nearly always by appointment . . . Monsieur doesn't need to do that, you understand?'

'Drink up, Monsieur Maigret, and let me refill your glass.'

He drained it and they all clinked glasses again. Francis and La Popine were both slightly overwhelmed by Maigret's gravity, by the huge effort he was making and which they vaguely sensed.

'It's so hard,' said La Popine, as if to console him, 'to know what goes on in those big houses . . . People like us, we say what we think and even more . . . but others—'

'Look,' broke in Francis. 'Just take this evening, for instance . . . Usually, I wait for Monsieur to ring for his whisky . . . Every night, at around ten, when he is in his library, he has a nightcap . . . Even though I have a room in the house, he knows that I don't sleep there . . . I put the tray down on the desk, I put the ice in the glass, and invariably he says to me: "Good night, Francis . . . you may go . . ."'

'Tonight . . .'

He sensed that Maigret was tense and it made him awkward, as if he were afraid of letting him down once again.

'It's only a detail . . . It came back to me because La Popine just said that you never know what's going on in big houses . . . Usually, I prepare the tray in advance and I sometimes sit there for a quarter of an hour watching the clock . . . I am alone at that moment . . . Jeanne is in her room, smoking cigarettes and reading novels in bed . . . The cook is married and sleeps in town. At ten fifteen when I realized that Monsieur hadn't rung for me, I quietly went upstairs with the tray . . . There was some light under the door . . . I waited for a while, then I looked through the keyhole . . . He wasn't in his chair . . . I knocked but I saw no one. I went into every room, except Madame's bedroom, of course, but he was nowhere to be found . . . Not downstairs, nor in his consulting room in the annexe . . . I went up to Jeanne's room and she told me that he wasn't in Madame's room either, and that her door was locked.'

'Just a moment . . . Is the door usually locked?'

'Not when Monsieur is out . . . Mind you, I didn't think anything of it and, at half past ten I put the tray out for him and left . . . It's the first time he's ever gone out without telling me. What's more, he'd left his light on.'

'Are you sure he had gone out?'

'His hat wasn't on the coat stand.'

'Did he take the car?'

'No, I looked in the garage . . .'

Just then, La Popine and Francis both stared at Maigret,

at first surprised, then anxious as he stood up, his face inscrutable.

'Do you have a telephone?' he asked.

He had to go into the shop and lean on the icy marble counter, next to the enamel scales.

'Hello! . . . Is that the Brasserie du Remblai? . . . Tell me . . . Have you seen Doctor Bellamy this evening?'

They didn't ask who was calling.

'No, not this afternoon . . . After dinner, that's right . . . You haven't seen him? . . . Just a moment, please . . . Is the chief inspector there by any chance? . . . He never comes in the evening? . . . Don't hang up, mademoiselle . . . Am I talking to the waiter? . . . The manager? . . . None of the gentlemen who play bridge are there? . . . Yes. Monsieur Rouillet, Monsieur Lourceau . . . Right . . . Put Monsieur Lourceau on, would you? . . .'

A languid voice on the other end, that of a man who is on his fifth or sixth hour of bridge and at least his sixth little tipple.

'Hello! Monsieur Lourceau . . . I'm sorry to disturb you . . . Chief Inspector Maigret . . . It doesn't matter . . . I'd like a simple piece of information . . . Do you know where I'm likely to find Bellamy at this hour? . . . No, he's not at home . . . Really? . . . He never goes out at night? . . . You have no idea? . . . Thank you very much . . .'

He became increasingly heavy, and there was a hint of anxiety in his eyes. He flicked through the telephone directory and called the coroner.

'Hello . . . Inspector Maigret here . . . No, it's not about an investigation . . . I would simply like to know whether

Doctor Bellamy is with you . . . I thought that, given what's happened and since you are friends . . . No, no! . . . I simply need to ask him something . . . You haven't seen him? . . . You haven't the least idea where I might be able to get hold of him? . . . What? . . . At the hospital? . . . I hadn't thought of that.'

It was so straightforward! Might not the doctor have gone to the hospital to see one of his patients?

'Hello . . . Sister Aurélie? . . . I'm sorry . . . I thought I recognized her voice . . . Can you tell me whether Doctor Bellamy . . .'

Neither at the convent hospital nor at the municipal hospital.

'One thing, Francis . . . Does the doctor's bedroom overlook Le Remblai?'

'Not exactly . . . It looks on to the east façade, but you can see it from the promenade.'

'Thank you very much.'

'Are you going?'

He left them completely baffled in their little dining room, Francis in his slippers and his open shirt, La Popine thrilled to have spent an evening with her idol.

'If you are in the neighbourhood tomorrow lunchtime, Monsieur Maigret, I'll be bound to have some information about the girl . . .'

He was barely listening. By now the streets were completely empty. It was past midnight. He spotted a police officer under a gas lamp and almost stopped him to ask whether he had seen Doctor Bellamy.

In the big house on Le Remblai, the only lit window was

that of the library. Francis had left the light on when he went home, as he had told Maigret. If the doctor had come back, there would probably be a light on in his room. In any case, he would have switched off the light in his study after drinking his whisky.

La Popine had spoken of a small town. But right now, Maigret found it too big. Big enough, in any case, for it to be impossible to locate a man and a girl in it.

If only he had known Lucile's name earlier!

He walked with great, rapid strides. Instead of going back to his hotel, he took a detour and saw the red light of the police station where only a sergeant and a few officers were on duty.

'Do any of you happen to know a girl called Lucile?'

They broke off their game of belote, looked at each other and racked their brains.

'My wife's called Lucile,' joked one of them, 'but, since you said a girl, it can't be her . . .'

'You don't know her surname?' the sergeant asked naively.

It was an officer of around thirty who taught Maigret a lesson, saying slowly:

'That's a question you should be asking the schoolmistresses.'

Of course! Maigret, who had never had any children, hadn't thought of that. It was so simple!

'How many schools are there in Les Sables d'Olonne?'

'Hold on a minute . . . If you count Château d'Oléron, that makes three. I'm talking about girls' schools . . . Not including the convent schools . . .'

'Do the teachers sleep there?'

'Of course not . . . Especially as it's the summer holidays now . . .'

Maigret had conducted thousands of investigations, nosed around in the most diverse milieus. But just as, a few days earlier, he had known nothing of nuns or the atmosphere of a hospital, he was equally ignorant of everything to do with schools.

'Do you think the teachers have the telephone?'

'It's unlikely . . . They earn about as little as we do, poor things!'

Suddenly, he was weary. Since five o'clock that afternoon, his mind had been working so fast that he suddenly felt drained, useless, just as he hit a blank wall.

Eight or ten schoolteachers were asleep somewhere in the town, in those little houses huddled together, their windows open on to narrow streets or little gardens.

One of them at least knew Lucile, whose homework she marked every day.

At one point, on the threshold of the police station, about to step out into the dark again, he had a moment's hesitation and nearly went back inside to ask for the list of all the local schoolmistresses, then go from door to door.

Was it the feeling that he was being absurd that stopped him?

The town isn't so big, La Popine had said.

Too big, unfortunately! They must have been talking about him as they fell asleep, the fishmonger and Francis! Perhaps that other couple too, the Flemish woman and Fernand, the butcher! And Lourceau, the coroner, the nun on night duty at the convent hospital, all the people he had bothered that evening.

He had probably left a trail of anxiety behind him, or at least curiosity.

Did he have the right, because he had a vague hunch, to disturb more streets, to disturb this entire little town nestling around its port?

He rang at the door of his hotel. Monsieur Léonard, who had waited up for him snoozing in a chair, came and opened it, a mute reproach in his eyes. Not because he had been kept up, but because he assumed that Maigret had been misbehaving.

'You look tired,' he said. 'A little drink, before you go upstairs?'

'You don't happen to know a girl called Lucile who . . .'

This was ridiculous. He was annoyed with himself. Monsieur Léonard filled two small glasses with Calvados. Good Lord! How many little tipples and glasses of white wine had Maigret drunk over the past few days! Even so, he wasn't drunk.

'To your good health!'

He stumbled up the stairs and dropped his clothes casually on the floor of his room. The next day, or rather the same day, as it was past midnight, would be the funeral. Beforehand, he would make a telephone call to Chief Inspector Mansuy, who was in his office from eight o'clock in the morning.

The first part of the night went by in a sort of nightmare. He rang doorbells, hundreds of doorbells, and heads appeared around half-open doors, heads that shook from left to right and right to left in negation. No one spoke. Neither did he. And yet everyone understood that he was looking for the doctor and Lucile.

Then a big, dark void, nothingness, and finally a knocking on his door, the voice of Germaine, the chambermaid:

'You're wanted on the telephone . . .'

He had gone to bed without putting on his pyjamas and had to hunt for them everywhere. His pillow was damp with an acrid sweat that smelled of alcohol. He did not hear the familiar noises in the adjacent rooms. It was either too early or too late.

He slipped on his dressing gown as he opened the door.

'What time is it?'

'Half past seven.'

Time seemed out of joint. He did not recognize the usual morning light. And why was Chief Inspector Mansuy calling him at half past seven?

'Hello! . . . Is that you, sir?'

Mansuy's voice also sounded strange.

'We've found out the surname . . .'

A silence. Why didn't Maigret dare ask any questions?

'She's called Lucile Duffieux . . .'

Another silence. Time and space were definitely out of order.

'Well?' he barked, exasperated.

'*She's dead . . .*'

Then, still holding the receiver, Maigret felt his eyes fill with tears.

'*She was strangled last night, in her bed, next to her mother's bedroom . . .*'

Monsieur Léonard, who was coming out of the cellar, a bottle of white wine in his hand, stood there bemused, wondering why Maigret was looking at him so fiercely and seemed not to recognize him.

5.

It was already late morning when Maigret noticed that the sky was grey and that a few drops of rain had probably fallen at dawn. Until then, the greyness of people and things, added to his own greyness, had stopped him from looking at the sky and noticing that, for the first time since his arrival at Les Sables d'Olonne, the sea was a murky green, its surface ruffled, almost black in places.

At the police station, the officers on night duty hadn't been relieved yet, and there was an atmosphere of disarray, tiredness and disquiet. At the foot of the stairs, he bumped into the officer who, at around midnight, had had the idea of contacting a schoolmistress. What age were his own daughters? Recognizing Maigret, he started. His tunic was unbuttoned, his hair tousled. He had slept on a bench. And now, standing in front of him, was the man who, a few hours earlier, had been desperately trying to find out where the girl lived.

It didn't make sense. Nothing made sense that morning. Did the officer think that Maigret was the killer?

Maigret lumbered up the stairs. His pipe tasted stale. He had shaved and dressed in haste, had found waiting outside the police car that Mansuy had sent for him so as to save time. Why had he asked the driver to take a detour via Le Remblai?

Probably to get a glimpse of the doctor's house. It was in its usual place, of course. The entire first floor seemed quiet, the shutters were closed, but decorators were hanging black drapes around the front door. He also drove past the church, this time because it was on the way, and there was only a handful of elderly women in starched headdresses coming out of Low Mass.

There was a certain febrility in the inspectors' office. Several of them were on the telephone. There was incredulity in every pair of eyes. The disgruntled faces were not simply expressing annoyance at having been dragged from sleep too early, but contained shock and a muted anger.

Most of the men were unshaven. They could not have been there long. Perhaps they had found a bar open on the way and managed to grab a coffee?

The door at the back opened. Mansuy had been watching out for Maigret's arrival and stood waiting for him in the doorway to his office, so changed that Maigret felt somewhat awkward.

Who knows? Perhaps Mansuy felt the same about him. The chief inspector had not shaved either. He had been the first to be informed. The first on the scene. People were surprised to see his cheeks invaded by a thick stubble, as pervasive as couch grass, a darker auburn than his hair.

It was no longer timidity that Maigret read in his pale blue eyes, but a genuine anxiety. Maigret advanced towards him and went in. The door closed behind him. And the stocky chief inspector's eyes remained riveted on him, asking a silent question.

Maigret was too caught up in his own thoughts to worry about other people's reactions. How could Mansuy not be intimidated by this burly man who, the previous evening, had been obstinately trying to track down this girl whom no one had ever heard of, giving a detailed description of her, just a few hours before she was strangled in her bed?

'I presume you want to go over there?' he said hoarsely.

There weren't many opportunities at Les Sables d'Olonne to see such sights, and it had left him deeply upset. Maigret could tell from the way he had said 'over there'.

'I managed to get hold of the public prosecutor's office at La Roche-sur-Yon on the telephone. The prosecutor will arrive at around eleven. Perhaps before, if they manage to gather his men earlier. He insisted on asking the Poitiers Flying Squad to send two inspectors over. I didn't tell him that you were here. I thought that best. Was that right?'

'It was right.'

'Won't you be handling the investigation?'

Maigret shrugged without replying, and he could tell Mansuy was disappointed. What could he do?

'There's a crowd outside the house, even though it's still early. It's on the outskirts of town, a whole neighbourhood of little houses surrounded by small gardens. Old Duffieux is night watchman in the shipyards. He took the job after he'd had his arm amputated. You'll meet him. It must have been terrible for him. This is what happened . . .'

Mansuy told Maigret the story, his elbows on the desk, his chin resting on his fists.

'He left work at six in the morning, as soon as the first crew arrived. Everything was as usual that morning, absolutely everything. He's a calm, meticulous man. The housewives who rise early can set their watches by the time he walks past. He goes quietly home, at around six twenty. He told me all this in detail, sounding like a sleepwalker. The front door opens directly into the kitchen. There's a chair to the left, a straw-bottomed chair, you'll see it. His slippers are waiting by the chair.

'He takes off his shoes, so as not to wake anyone. He puts a match in the stove, where the fire has been laid, with a sheet of newspaper and kindling . . .

'The ground coffee is in the filter of the cafetière and, as soon as the water in the kettle boils, he pours it over. All he needs to do is put two lumps of sugar in the floral bowl.

'You'll see . . . By the fireside is a clock with a brass pendulum . . .

'It is six thirty on the clock when, a bowl in his hand, he creeps silently into his wife's bedroom.

'For years, each morning, it's been the same routine . . .'

Maigret opened the window, even though the morning air was cool.

'Go on . . .'

'Madame Duffieux is a pale, sickly woman. She never recovered from the birth of her last child, which doesn't stop her from trotting around from dawn till dusk . . . She's a tall and anxious woman, always tense, always agitated, one of those women who spend their lives expecting disaster to strike . . .

'She got dressed while her husband took off his heavy

night clothes. She commented: "It's raining . . . It rained earlier . . .'"

It was only then that Maigret looked at the sky, which was still grey.

'The two of them sat together for half an hour. It's pretty much their only moment of intimacy.

'Then, on the dot of seven, Duffieux opened a door to go and wake up his daughter.

'Those little houses don't have shutters. The window at the back overlooking the garden was wide open, as always at this time of year.

'Lucile was dead in her bed, her face a bluish colour, with big black bruises on her neck . . .

'Shall we go over there?'

But he didn't get up yet. He was waiting. He was still waiting. He couldn't believe that Maigret had nothing to tell him.

'Let's go,' was all Maigret said, with a sigh.

And the street of the outlying district was exactly as he had imagined it from Mansuy's description. It was indeed the sort of street that girls like Lucile come from, with a corner shop that sells vegetables, groceries, kerosene and sweets, and where the women are on their doorsteps and children play on the pavements.

There were huddles in the doorways. Women still in their nightdresses had simply slipped a coat around their shoulders.

Fifty or so people clustered around a little house just like the others, where a uniformed police officer stood on guard. The car stopped and the two men alighted.

Then, standing on the pavement, Maigret paused for a moment, abruptly, for no apparent reason, the way people with heart disease sometimes stop in the street.

'Do you want to go in?'

He nodded. The curious onlookers stood aside to let them through. Mansuy tapped discreetly on the door . . . It was the man who opened it. His eyes weren't red, but he looked dazed and he walked mechanically. He glanced at Mansuy, whom he recognized, and took no further notice of them.

That day, the house seemed no longer to belong to him. A bedroom door was open and a shape lay on the bed letting out a regular, animal moan. It was Madame Duffieux. A local doctor sat at her bedside, while an old woman with a paunch, a neighbour perhaps, was bustling around the oven.

The floral bowls were still on the table, one full of coffee, the one Duffieux had taken in to his daughter at seven o'clock.

The house had only three rooms. To the right, the kitchen, which was also the sitting room and was fairly large, with one window overlooking the garden and another with a view of the street. To the left, two doors, two bedrooms, the parents' room at the front, and the other at the back.

There were photographs on the walls and on the mantelpiece.

'Did they have just the one child?' asked Maigret softly.

'I believe they have a son, but I don't think he's in Les Sables d'Olonne. I confess I didn't have the courage to question them at length. The prosecutor will be here later, and the gentlemen from Poitiers will do what must be done . . .'

Mansuy thus admitted that he wasn't born for this job. He covertly watched Maigret, who seemed afraid to go into the second bedroom, whose door was closed.

'No one has touched anything?' he said, automatically, because it was the professional thing to ask.

Mansuy shook his head.

'Let's go in . . .'

He pushed open the door and was surprised to catch a strong whiff of tobacco. Then he spotted a man silhouetted against the window, who turned to them.

'I left one of my men in this room as a precaution,' said Mansuy.

'You promised to relieve me,' protested the officer.

'A bit later, Larrouy.'

There were two beds in the room, and between them just room for a bedside table. The beds were of iron, the black bars standing out against the bluish wallpaper. The bed against the left-hand wall had not been slept in. On the other, a huddled form was entirely covered with a sheet.

A big wardrobe stood against the opposite wall, and there was a table covered with a towel, with a white enamel basin on it, a comb, a brush, soap and a saucer; and, under the table, a pitcher of water and a blue enamel pail. That was all. This was Lucile's room, which she must have shared with her brother.

'Do you know who the old lady is, in the kitchen?'

'She wasn't there this morning. Or if she was, I didn't see her, because the place was full of curious folk and we had a job getting them out.'

'Did the mother not hear anything?'

'Nothing.'

'Has the coroner been?'

'He must have come by because I telephoned him before coming myself. I'll call him again once I'm back in the office.'

Maigret finally did what was expected of him. He walked slowly over to the bed and bent over to lift the sheet. He only looked for a few seconds and then went straight over to the window.

Mansuy stood close to him. The three men gazed out at the little garden surrounded by pickets linked together by barbed wire. In one corner was a rabbit hutch, in the other, a shed where Duffieux must keep his tools and probably pottered about in his free time. A few vegetables grew in the sandy soil, pale green leeks, lettuces, cabbages. Five tomato plants tied to stakes bore their red fruits.

They did not need to speak. This was how the man had got in. It was easy to climb over the barbed wire, even easier to clamber over the window-sill. Beyond the garden was a patch of waste ground and, further away, some disused buildings which must once have been a factory.

'If he left any footprints,' said the inspector quietly, 'this morning's rain will have washed them away. My colleague Charbonnet had a look . . .'

He sought the approval of Maigret, who didn't move a muscle. Had he ever bothered with footprints?

He went into the garden, however, through the kitchen

where two people had just arrived. There was a little path made of flat stones scavenged from the waste ground. The rabbits watched him, wrinkling their noses, and he grabbed a handful of cabbage leaves, opened the hutch and closed it again.

This greyness was so typical of the squalid surroundings in which women like Madame Duffieux, thin and sickly, spent their lives counting out every single sou.

'What time is it?' he asked, without thinking to take his watch out of his pocket.

'Five to nine.'

'The funeral is due to take place at ten thirty, isn't it?'

It took Mansuy a second to understand, the idea of a funeral becoming confused in his mind with the small body they had just seen. Then he remembered the other dead girl, and looked at Maigret more attentively.

'Are you going?'

'Yes.'

'Do you think there's a connection?'

Had Maigret heard? He did not appear to have. He returned slowly to the kitchen. The old woman, sighing deeply and continually wiping her eyes on the corner of her apron, was telling the newcomers about the tragedy, a brother of Duffieux's and his wife, who had been informed by neighbours. It was odd, these people spoke loudly, with coarse language which was very graphic, without giving any thought to the mother lying in the next room whose door was open, so that her moans accompanied the old woman's account like a monotonous chant:

'I said to Gérard: "It can only be a madman . . ."

'Because I knew the girl, better than anyone perhaps – she used to come and play at my house when she was little and I gave her the doll that belonged to my daughter who passed away . . .'

'Excuse me one moment . . .'

Maigret touched her on the shoulder. She suddenly became respectful. For her, all those she saw that day in the house were gentlemen, official figures.

'Has the son been informed?'

'Émile?'

She darted a look at one of the portraits on the wall, that of a young man of seventeen or eighteen, with delicate features, sharp eyes, dressed with a certain elegance.

'You don't know that Émile's left? That's what's so dreadful for this poor woman, your honour . . . Her son who went off last week . . . Her daughter who—'

'Is he in the army?'

Wasn't that the tragedy of this sort of people?

'No, no, my good sir . . . He isn't old enough for the army yet . . . Hold on . . . He must be nineteen and a half now . . . He earned a good living here . . . His employers thought very highly of him . . . Then, would you believe, he gets it into his head to go and live in Paris! . . . Without warning, just like that! . . . Without telling anyone! . . . He didn't even leave a note . . . He simply said he had to work all night . . . Marthe believed him . . . She believes everything people tell her . . .

'In the morning, seeing that he hadn't come home, curiosity made her look in her son's wardrobe, and she saw that all his things had gone . . .'

'Then, when the postman came by, he brought a letter in which Émile asked her forgiveness, telling her that he was going to Paris, that it was his life, his future, and I don't know what else . . . She read it to me . . . It must be in the drawer of the dresser . . .'

She made to go and fetch it; Maigret put up his hand to stop her.

'You don't know what day that was?'

'Just a moment . . . I can tell you . . .'

She went into the bedroom and spoke in a low voice to Duffieux, who stared at her uncomprehending, and then glanced over at Maigret. He wondered why he was being asked this question, cast his mind back and replied:

'It must have been Tuesday . . . Tuesday night.'

'Do you know if they have heard from him since?'

'The day before yesterday Marthe showed me a picture postcard she received from Paris.'

Chief Inspector Mansuy did not attempt to understand. He still watched Maigret uncomfortably, as if he suspected him of having some sort of fiendish power. He half expected to learn, during the course of the day, that the son too was dead.

As they came out of the house, a tall, young man in a gabardine raincoat was elbowing his way through the curious onlookers.

'A journalist,' announced Mansuy.

Maigret preferred to make a quick getaway. The contemptible game was beginning, the journalists, the photographers, the prosecutor, then the gentlemen from Poitiers and their interrogations, the forensics experts cluttering up the little rooms with their equipment and photographing the girl's body from all angles.

'Were you expecting it?' Mansuy finally dared ask in the car on the way back to the police station.

And Maigret, who seemed far away:

'I was expecting something . . .'

'Will you come up to my office for a moment?'

The police station was beginning to return to normal, filled with people who needed a certificate, a signature, some document or other, full of poor wretches waiting on benches until it suited these gentlemen to see them. Every officer was asking for Mansuy, but he went straight up to the first floor.

'Poitiers telephoned,' an inspector informed him. 'They're sending you Piéchaud and Boivert. They left over an hour ago by car and will be here at around ten. Forensics are with them. They asked us to put a cordon around the town and to arrest all the suspects.'

Mansuy replied:

'That's already been done.'

As he said this, he darted Maigret a sheepish look as if to say:

'What else can I do? It's pointless, but that's standard procedure and I have to follow it.'

'Has Doctor Jamar not telephoned?'

'Not yet.'

'Get him on the phone . . . At this hour he's probably at the hospital.'

He was the coroner, who was also a consultant at the municipal hospital.

'Doctor Jamar? Mansuy here . . . Yes . . . Yes . . . I understand . . . The prosecutor will be here at around eleven . . . I think it's best you don't trouble yourself to come again until I call you, because these gentlemen are very likely to be late . . . I'll telephone you and it will only take you a minute to drive over . . . Of course . . . Between eleven p.m. and two a.m.? . . . Thank you . . . No, I'm not in charge of the investigation . . . I'm waiting for Poitiers . . . What? . . .'

A glance at Maigret. Hesitation.

'I don't think he's handling it . . . In any case, not officially.'

'Very good.' Maigret gave an approving nod.

He had understood. He could have repeated verbatim the coroner's words even though he hadn't heard them. A superficial examination was not sufficient to establish the time of death other than very approximately.

Between eleven p.m. and two a.m.

'Are you leaving?'

'I'm going to the funeral.'

'I'll try to drop by for a moment, either at the Bellamys' house or at the church, but I wonder if I'll have the time. Give Bellamy my apologies . . .'

Another anxious glance in Maigret's direction, especially as he uttered the word 'apologies', but Maigret remained impassive.

'See you later . . .'

'If the gentlemen from Poitiers mention you . . .'

'Tell them I'm here on holiday.'

It was still too early to go to the Bellamys', but he was keen to head towards the quayside first. Not to drink.

True, he went into one of his usual cafés and downed a glass, but it was La Popine he wanted to see. Her shop was full of people. Her sleeves rolled up, Francis's mistress plunged her plump rosy arms into the baskets of fish and shellfish and weighed them, ringing up the totals on her cash register.

'And for you, darling?'

She spoke to all her customers in a familiar tone, her eyes so bright, her complexion so fresh, that on this grey morning she made everything around her look enticing.

'You're telling me, girl! . . . The animal who did a thing like that . . . If ever I get my hands on him, I'll . . . scratch his eyes out. What's more, *I* think . . .'

She spotted Maigret, finished weighing, wiped her hands on her apron and called the maid:

'Take over for a minute, Mélanie . . . Come through here, Monsieur Maigret . . .'

And once in the little dining room redolent of cooking aromas:

'Do you think he's the one who killed her? . . . Who would have thought it last night, while the three of us were sitting there chatting? . . . If only you'd told me it was Marthe's daughter . . . We went to school together . . . Though not for long . . .'

'Do you know Madame Bellamy's maid?'

'Jeanne? I do believe I know her, even though she doesn't want to know me any more. I used to see her hanging around barefoot in the streets. Her mother works in the sardine cannery. They put her there too, at the age of thirteen, then she started working as a lady's maid. Since she's been working at the doctor's, she thinks she's too good to talk to anyone. Ask Francis—'

'You don't know where I could have a word with her?'

'It won't be easy anywhere other than in the house. She hasn't had anything to do with her mother since she remarried. She doesn't go dancing. She's besotted with her employer. She pampers and cossets her, she'd sleep on her floor if she was allowed. She barely deigns to answer when Francis speaks to her . . . So tell me! . . . Are you going to arrest the doctor?'

'I think that's out of the question . . . Thank you very much.'

'You'll be back, won't you? . . . This isn't the best time to talk . . . If you want to drop by for a drink this evening . . . I'm dying to know what's going to happen . . .'

But she was soft-hearted and would probably have inflicted the punishment she had threatened in the shop if she were to come face to face with the murderer.

The holidaymakers on the beach were oblivious of what had happened, and it was the usual scene with mothers and children in bathing costumes, sunshades and red and blue beach balls, and swimmers plunging into the water on the fringes of the waves.

By contrast, on the promenade, people dressed in black could be seen heading towards Doctor Bellamy's house. They were the local people of Les Sables d'Olonne. They greeted each other on the pavement with handshakes, formed little huddles, checked their watches, and went through the doorway draped with black curtains with silver tears.

Maigret recognized Monsieur Lourceau, a man called

Perrette, other regulars from the café who had already presented their condolences and were chatting quietly.

He too went inside. They had not needed to convert one of the reception rooms into a chapel of rest, since the entrance hall was spacious enough. You could no longer see the staircase, or the doors, the hall was in darkness with candles burning around a sumptuous coffin surrounded by an abundance of white flowers.

Philippe Bellamy, alone in leading the mourning, stood motionless, and one by one the visitors filed past and bowed their heads before him, having dipped a boxwood sprig in the holy water.

He was even more imposing thus, with only the white of his shirt front, collar and cuffs showing. His features seemed more delicate, more chiselled. He acknowledged each person's condolences with the same inclination of his head and neck, then he straightened up and looked each new arrival in the eye.

Maigret filed past like the others and also bowed, to find the same gaze directed at him. He did not discern any discomfort in it. Nothing indicated that for Bellamy he was anything other than one entity among so many other entities.

The sub-prefect arrived in his car and parked a few houses further along; the mayor and his deputy were also there, and all the town's bigwigs; no doubt they were discussing the girl's death.

The hearse arrived. Then it was the procession, which took a while to form, the slow march to the church with its doors draped in black.

The men took their seats to the right and, here again, Doctor Bellamy was alone in the front pew. In the second, among his friends, Maigret recognized the man of a certain age who, the previous evening, had been accompanying Madame Godreau.

She sat on the left, veiled and in full mourning. She constantly dabbed her face with a fine handkerchief whose perfume wafted over Maigret above that of the incense.

An organist had come all the way from La Roche-sur-Yon. There was also a baritone, and a children's choir. The church had gradually filled and the offering procession went on for around fifteen minutes.

The catafalque blocked Maigret's view of Madame Bellamy, the doctor's mother, who sat beside Madame Godreau and whose walking stick could occasionally be heard scraping the flagstones.

Odette Bellamy wasn't there. Francis filed past at the same time as the cook. Jeanne, the maid, had probably stayed back at the house with her mistress.

By the time they emerged from the church, the sun had come out, giving the street such a familiar look that it took a few moments to tune back into the mood of the town.

Then it was the long walk to the cemetery where Maigret, from a distance, glimpsed his colleague Mansuy, sweating, his cheeks still unshaven. He had managed, not without difficulty, to put in a brief appearance.

A few close friends accompanied Bellamy back to the gates. He got into Doctor Bourgeois' car, which would probably drive him back to his house.

Was there a family gathering? Were Madame Godreau

and her companion invited into the white house on Le Remblai?

Maigret couldn't find Mansuy and had to make his way back to the centre of town on foot. When he glanced at his watch, it was ten past midday. He realized he had forgotten something, that he had forgotten a sacred ritual. And he had no idea that this omission was causing quite a drama.

At the hospital, Madame Maigret had been given permission to get out of bed for the first time. She wasn't walking yet, but for an hour, no longer – the doctor had been insistent – she had been put in a wheelchair. For the first time, too, she had been able to wander through the corridors, glimpse other wards, the faces of the people who, before that, she had only heard talking, or moaning.

She and Sister Marie des Anges had plotted a little conspiracy, in whispers so as not to upset Mademoiselle Rinquet, who was more tight-lipped than ever. They were planning to surprise Maigret, who always telephoned on the dot of eleven. There was a telephone at the end of the corridor, in the visitors' room with vast bay windows which was known as the solarium.

Sister Aurélie was in on the secret. As soon as Monsieur 6 called, instead of answering, she would transfer the call to the visitors' room and Maigret would be astonished to hear his wife's voice on the other end of the line.

The wheelchair was in position fifteen minutes early. But at eleven thirty Sister Marie des Anges insisted on taking the patient back to her room.

By midday, a disappointed Madame Maigret was back

in bed and the nun tried to cheer her up, without success, while a triumphant smile hovered on Mademoiselle Rinquet's pursed lips.

'There are two gentlemen waiting for you. They say they're friends of yours. As they're in a hurry, they've already ordered lunch. They asked me for two rooms, but I don't have any vacancies.'

And Monsieur Léonard almost begged:

'You will have a little aperitif, won't you?'

The two men eating at Maigret's table were Piéchaud and Boivert, the Flying Squad inspectors, who had both worked with him. They rose as one, their napkins in their hands.

'Excuse us, chief . . . We've just got time for a bite before the prosecutor gets here.'

'I thought he was supposed be here at eleven?'

'He would have been if they'd been able to find the examining magistrate, but he was in the country . . . The people he was having lunch with don't have a telephone and we had to call the town hall, who sent the local policeman . . . In short, they'll all be here in an hour . . . Will you be joining us?'

Someone – perhaps Mansuy? – must have talked to them about Maigret's behaviour, for they exchanged knowing looks.

'Joining you for what?'

'You're on holiday, of course, we know that . . . Don't we, Boivert?'

One was around thirty, the other thirty-five. They were

experienced policemen, both of them. Men who knew their job, as they said at Quai des Orfèvres. Piéchaud, the older one, had almost been killed during the arrest of a Pole, and his right cheek bore the scar of a bullet wound.

Maigret sat down, distracted, and unfolded his napkin. He helped himself to the hors-d'oeuvre, only half listening to what his companions were saying.

'You already know that the girl wasn't raped? . . . At first glance, that's what it looked like . . . The crime of a sadist . . . That's what they told us at Poitiers. The local police have arrested a good half-dozen vagrants . . . It's incredible how many there are in the area . . . Only, if it had been that simple, you wouldn't have been on to the case since the day before, right?'

They were determined to worm it out of him.

'As far as we're concerned, we'd like nothing better than to work with you . . . Neither Boivert nor I know the town . . . In other words . . .'

Faced with Maigret's silence, Piéchaud was stumped.

'It's as you wish! . . . But surely, as the gentlemen from the prosecutor's office know you're here . . . I'd be surprised if they didn't insist on seeing you . . .'

'I am on holiday,' repeated Maigret, pouring himself a drink.

'Of course . . .'

'If I find anything out, I'll let you know . . .'

'You have always been on the level . . .'

He almost smiled. It was a very brief sunny interval. The clouds gathered over his brow again immediately. He wasn't hungry. He felt out of sorts, as if sickening for flu.

'In any case, if you want someone watched, or anything at all . . .'

'Thank you very much.'

'We've got to be off . . . It's time . . .'

In the corridor, Monsieur Léonard pointed out a little hotel where they might perhaps have a chance of getting a room. They exchanged glances again and, in the doorway, Piéchaud, the eldest, said:

'The chief's not exactly a bundle of laughs!'

6.

Maigret rang the hospital doorbell even though the time was not quite two thirty; he didn't take his watch from his pocket and didn't listen out for the sound of the bells ringing.

Sister Aurélie looked at him in almost reproachful surprise and was reluctant to pick up her telephone. He gave her a perfunctory smile which only flitted across his frowning, rather stubborn expression for a split second.

'I haven't come to see my wife,' he stated. 'I should like to speak with the mother superior first.'

'Are you sure, Monsieur 6, that it is the mother superior you need to see? It's the bursar sister who deals with all matters concerning the patients and the hospital in general, as well as any complaints . . .'

'Would you kindly inform the mother superior that Detective Chief Inspector Maigret wishes to speak to her?'

Sister Aurélie decided not to argue and, while she telephoned, he stared at the overly smooth walls, the too highly polished stairs, with a sort of resentment.

'Someone will come to fetch you,' said the nun.

'Thank you very much.'

He paced up and down the entrance hall, his hands behind his back, furious in advance at the thought he would be kept waiting. On turning round, he was utterly flabbergasted to see before him a nun he did not know waiting for him.

'Would you like to follow me, monsieur?'

Not up the stairs. At the back of the entrance hall, they went through a nail-studded oak door into another realm, even more cocoon-like, more silent than the hospital. The nuns must be wearing felt- or rubber-soled shoes, for their footsteps were completely silent. Twice, as they made their way through a maze of corridors, he looked over his shoulder on hearing behind him the vague swish of voluminous robes, the sway of rosaries, perhaps the air being displaced. The nuns sweeping around made him think of bats.

He glimpsed a chapel with artificial flowers on the altar. Then he was shown into a visitors' room where black chairs with crimson velvet seats lined the walls.

'Our Reverend Mother will be with you right away . . .'

Again that swishing of skirts, the clicking of rosary beads, the air being displaced by winged cornettes.

'Monsieur . . .?'

He shuddered, because the other nuns had only been mere nuns, whereas this one, even though she wore the same habit and, like the others, kept her hands hidden inside her wide sleeves, was a woman, a woman whose age and social milieu he could have fathomed.

Tall and slim, classy, she directed the calm gaze of her grey eyes at him.

'I haven't come to see you about my wife, Sister . . .'

He suspected he should have said Reverend Mother or something like that, but those words stuck in his throat.

'I wish to speak to Sister Marie des Anges for a few moments . . .'

Whereas he had thought she would be taken aback, she looked at him with the same imperturbable calm, and he was already beginning to detest her.

'You know, monsieur, that the rules—'

'Forgive me, Sister, but there's no question of rules today.'

He turned slightly red, because he had been the first to lose his composure.

'I was about to say that the rules,' she continued, 'only permit you to meet one of our sisters in the presence of another sister.'

'Even if I came with a warrant from an examining magistrate?'

He had promised himself that he'd be diplomatic, but this tall, bourgeois woman in a cornet irritated him, although he didn't know why. Or rather yes, he did know. As he spoke with the mother superior, the 'gentlemen' from the prosecutor's office were stomping around the Duffieux family's little house with the inspectors. They had done nothing either, other than work all their lives and count every sou. Their young daughter had been murdered in her bed and, instead of leaving them to their grief, the police had questioned them without compunction about the most private aspects of their lives, while nosey onlookers glued their faces to the windows and journalists subjected them to the continual bombardment of magnesium flashguns. So?

'Sister Marie des Anges is very young, monsieur, very easily upset.'

He merely shrugged.

'I'll send for her.'

She left the room and said a few words to a nun who must have been standing outside the door, for she was back almost immediately.

'I was expecting your visit. Sister Marie des Anges confessed to me yesterday. She committed a very serious infraction of the rules in writing that note to you without talking to me about it.'

He was stunned, disconcerted, on learning that the mother superior knew about the note.

'It is by chance, accidentally if you like, that she kept watch for an hour or two in room 15. She is not yet used to seriously ill patients and she was deeply affected by the girl's delirium.'

Warily, Maigret asked:

'Do you know Doctor Bellamy?'

'I know him.'

'I mean, do you know him purely as a doctor, or have you met him socially?'

Because they must both belong to the same world.

'I only know him as a doctor. I am from Bordeaux. Since you request it, Sister Marie des Anges will repeat to you herself, verbatim, as I shall order her to do . . .'

She was the one, not him, giving the orders!

'. . . the words that she heard, or thought she heard. It is pointless harassing her with questions to refresh her memory. I have already done that. The words you will hear are no different from those spoken by many patients who are delirious. I fear, however, that someone who is unaware of this might be tempted to attach too much importance to them. Sister Marie des Anges rashly shouldered a terrible responsibility. In listening to her, you will take on another and I pray God to inspire you with wisdom and caution.'

There was a swishing in the corridor.

'Come in, Sister. I authorize you to repeat to Monsieur Maigret the words that you confided to me.'

'You may stay,' Maigret decided abruptly.

And, blushing, Sister Marie des Anges looked from one to the other.

'She was in a coma,' she stammered. 'Then once, while I was on duty, she was struggling as if to sit up, then she clutched my arm shouting:

'"Have they . . ."'

She faltered, seeking further approval from the mother superior. Maigret continued to look disgruntled.

'". . . Have they arrested him? . . . They mustn't arrest him . . . Do you hear? . . . I don't want . . . I don't want . . ."'

She broke off again. Maigret guessed that the most important part was yet to come and the mother superior came to her aid. It was she who said:

'Go on. You know that I wrote down the words you repeated to me and I will report them to the inspector if he so wishes.'

'She added:

'"You mustn't believe her . . . She's the monster . . ."'

'Is that all?'

'That's all I could understand at the time. There are even some words I'm not certain about.'

And yet she had not got everything off her chest. Maigret realized it from the questioning look that Sister Marie des Anges gave the mother superior.

'At other moments, did you catch any other words?'

'Yes . . . but they made no sense . . . She talked about a silver knife . . .'

'Are you sure about those two words?'

'Yes, because she said them several times . . . She also said: "*I touched it . . .*"'

'And she gave a great shudder.'

'Is that all, Sister?'

Calmly, in a gentle but firm voice, the mother superior said:

'You may go, Sister.'

Maigret frowned and was about to object. With the same calm, she signalled to him to keep quiet and went over and shut the door herself.

'The rest, which is of no interest by the way, I prefer to tell you myself. I cannot take it upon myself to force one of my youngest sisters to speak of certain things in the presence of a man. I don't know whether you have ever had the occasion to sit with patients who are raving.'

She dared ask this of Maigret, who had thirty years in the Police Judiciaire behind him!

'What I wish to emphasize is that sometimes there is a total change of personality. A doctor will explain it to you better than I. The fact is that several times foul language escaped the lips of this young woman, that you will forgive me for not repeating.'

'Did Sister Marie des Anges say these words to you?'

'It was my duty to hear her confession.'

'I presume that these words allude to sexual matters?'

'Most of them. I would add that they are words that cannot be found in the dictionary.'

He hesitated, and ended up bowing his head.

'Thank you very much,' he stuttered.

And, as if she were pardoning his earlier attitude, she spoke in a gentler tone to say:

'I expect that now you wish to see our dear patient who, from what I have heard, was disappointed not to receive your usual telephone call. To think that she had got out of bed and was thrilled to be answering in person.'

'Thank you very much,' he repeated as she preceded him down the long corridor.

The studded door opened and closed again behind him. He was shut out. He found himself back in the hospital which, in comparison with the convent proper, felt like a vulgar, noisy place.

It wasn't Sister Marie des Anges but Sister Aldegonde who was waiting for him at the top of the stairs. Madame Maigret looked at him with some apprehension, without daring to ask him any questions.

'Please forgive me,' he said. 'I was very busy this morning.'

'I know.'

'What do you know?'

'It's only just occurred to me. I presume you went to the funeral? Did you see our wreath?'

To think that it was his wife who was asking him that question! Two weeks in hospital had been enough to change her.

'You know, I'm a lot better—'

'And you got out of bed, yes.'

'Who told you?'

He did not dare mention the mother superior. He was impatient to get away. He didn't like the way Madame Maigret was looking at him. He tried hard to talk about everyday things in a cheerful voice.

Never had the thirty minutes seemed so long, especially since Sister Marie des Anges didn't relieve the tedium with her usual flitting in and out. When it was time for him to leave and he leaned over his wife to kiss her, she whispered:

'Are you busy with number 15?'

She had guessed, of course! She added with a hint of reproach, but without hope:

'You were so happy to have a holiday at last! Will you telephone me tomorrow?'

He had to turn back to say goodbye to Mademoiselle Rinquet, whom he had forgotten. An extraordinary thing, he walked all the way across town without stopping at a single bar. It was from his hotel that he telephoned:

'Hello! . . . I'd like to speak to Doctor Bellamy, please . . . Hello! . . . Is that you, doctor? . . . Forgive me for disturbing you . . . I wouldn't expect to find you at the café today . . . I would like, however, to have a conversation with you, at whatever time suits you best . . . Hello! . . . Sorry? . . . Right away? . . . Thank you . . . I'll be at your house in ten minutes . . .'

Again, he forgot to greet Monsieur Léonard, who hung around him with the expression of a dog wondering why his master doesn't stroke him any more.

'Supposing the gentlemen ask me where you are?' he ventured.

'Tell them that you have no idea.'

He walked with great strides, his teeth clenched around the stem of his pipe. It was Francis who opened the door to him, and winked as he said:

'You're expected upstairs.'

The black drapes, candles and flowers were all gone. The house had returned to normal and only the smell of the chapel of rest lingered in the air. Maigret followed the butler up the thick stair carpet. Francis opened a door, that of the study, and, before seeing anything, Maigret caught a whiff of cigar smoke.

Two men were in the room, in an atmosphere of perfect privacy. One, standing, was Doctor Bellamy, sharp and precise, without the slightest hint of disquiet in his expression or in his voice.

'My dear Alain,' he said, with perhaps the slightest note of irony aimed at the visitor, 'I am delighted to introduce Chief Inspector Maigret, whom you were so keen to meet . . . Monsieur Maigret, may I introduce my old friend Alain de Folletier, examining magistrate at La Roche-sur-Yon . . .'

The man was tall, slightly rotund, and ruddy-faced. He was wearing a russet-coloured jacket, jodhpurs and fawn boots. He was the one smoking a cigar from the box lying open on the desk, beside the liqueur glasses.

'Delighted to meet you, inspector . . . I don't have to tell you why I am here today . . . Embarrassed, incidentally, to be in riding dress. I had taken a day off and gone riding with friends who live in the country . . . No one was able to get hold of me on the telephone and the prosecutor urged me to come at once, as I was . . .'

The doctor invited Maigret to sit in one of the leather armchairs and offered him a cigar.

'Chartreuse or Armagnac?'

He replied without thinking:

'Armagnac.'

But he did not take the cigar, filling his pipe instead. It was very hot in the room where he sensed that before his arrival the two men had been having an amicable conversation.

'We were at school together, Bellamy and I. Which explains why I was able to free myself from . . .'

From his duty! That's what he meant! From a prosecutor's visit to ordinary people of no importance, like the Duffieux family.

'As soon as I had finished with that business . . . You know about it, inspector? . . . I have been told that you were here, but on holiday . . .'

A sceptical smile hovered on the lips of the magistrate, who had a brown pencil moustache.

'That doesn't prevent you from knowing a lot of things, does it? . . . Or from refusing to help the inspectors from Poitiers . . . That's up to you . . . Mind you, I'm only teasing . . . I know you by reputation, as does everyone . . . When you telephoned, and Philippe suggested I wait for you, I was delighted to have the opportunity—'

'Did Doctor Bellamy also tell you why I wished to see him?'

There were three of them, one smoking a pipe, one smoking a cigar, and lastly the doctor who was smoking slim Egyptian cigarettes. The cut-glass decanters and glasses on the desk contained Chartreuse and vintage Armagnac.

'He has just informed me,' retorted the magistrate cheerfully. 'I find it rather amusing . . . It is typical of Philippe and, may I add, it is typical of you . . . Of you as one imagines you . . .'

The doctor was sitting down, his elbows on the desk, calmly looking from one man to the other.

'In short, if I have understood correctly, and despite your sacrosanct holiday, you thought there was something fishy about the accident of which his unfortunate sister-in-law was a victim and you started sniffing around him . . .'

The amicable tone with a hint of condescension was that of a gentleman of old stock conversing with a man who is interesting but rather common, a sort of character that he will tell his friends about later.

'The doctor told you that I'd been sniffing around him?'

'Not in so many words . . . He told me he had guessed your suspicions and had made things easy for you by placing himself at your disposal and inviting you here . . . Is that correct?'

'More or less.'

'That's him all over . . . He rather enjoys playing tricks like that on people . . . Since you telephoned him to ask to meet him, I presume you have some news? . . . Don't worry, Philippe, I'll be going . . . I am more conscious than anyone of the confidential nature of an investigation . . .'

'Do stay . . . Monsieur Maigret can speak . . .'

Maigret sat holding his glass. The armchair was so deep that he found himself hunched, his neck sunk into his broad shoulders.

'One of the things I should like to ask you, doctor, is where you went last night.'

It was fleeting, but there was a glance in the direction of the window. Bellamy was thinking of the light he had left on, probably to make people think he was at home. Was he also thinking of Francis? Possibly. The fact is, he replied simply:

'I paid a visit to my mother-in-law, at the Hôtel de Vendée.'

Maigret almost turned red. The magistrate smiled, as if he had scored a point.

'She arrived in the late afternoon yesterday with her husband, for she is legally remarried.'

Another point! Maigret pictured the couple he had spotted the previous day in the street. How had he failed to think of that. It was so simple!

'She telephoned me at around eight o'clock in the evening. I didn't want to put her to any trouble after her tiring journey so I went to the hotel and told her about the accident in more detail.'

'Thank you very much. May I take the liberty of asking you another question: who has been treating your wife since the 1st of August?'

'Doctor Bourgeois. I could have looked after her myself, since she is suffering from a nervous breakdown, but, like most of my fellow doctors, I am loath to treat a member of my own family.'

Folletier smiled, as he notched up another point. He was enjoying himself. This would make a great story to tell back at La Roche-sur-Yon and in the neighbouring chateaux.

'What date did you call Doctor Bourgeois?'

A barely perceptible hesitation, but the examining magistrate, who was stretching out his long, booted legs, seemed to sense something in the air.

'I don't remember.'

'The first day?'

'I don't think so. I presume, Monsieur Maigret, that you know what it's like to care for a sick person at home? I was forgetting that your wife is in hospital at the moment, being treated by my colleague Bertrand. Did you call him out on the first day?'

'The second.'

'Because symptoms were precise, because almost immediately your wife had a raging fever. In my wife's case—'

Folletier wanted to protest, out of gallantry, that there could be no question of infringing Madame Bellamy's privacy, and this time he glared at Maigret, whom he considered ill-bred.

'Let it go! In my wife's case, I was saying, it began with a state of exhaustion. She stayed in bed, as women so often do—'

'What date?'

'I didn't make a note.'

'It was two days before the accident, wasn't it?'

'It could have been.'

The magistrate's legs were twitching with impatience, with disapproval.

'Don't forget, doctor, that you're the one who invited me to come here whenever I wished to ask you all the questions I needed to ask.'

'Once again, be my guest.'

'Did Doctor Bourgeois come the day of the accident?'

'No.'

'The day after?'

'I don't think so.'

'So, at the earliest, two days afterwards. Did he come yesterday?'

'Yes.'

'Today?'

'Not yet.'

'Were you present at each visit?'

'Yes.'

'That's only natural, I think!' burst out Alain de Folletier. 'Allow me to say, inspector, that—'

'Forget it, Alain! Go on, Monsieur Maigret . . .'

Maigret had been staring for ages from a distance at the objects on the desk. The solid leather writing pad bore the doctor's monogram, as did the blotter. In front of the ink-well, there was a big ivory paper knife and another, slimmer one for opening letters.

'Would you permit me to ask your butler a simple question, in your presence of course?'

This time, the magistrate rose and, again, it was the doctor who pacified him with a gesture, while with the other hand he pressed an electric bell.

'You see,' he remarked with a hint of edginess, 'that I'm playing the game all the way.'

'Do you still think this is a game?'

There was a knock at the door. It was Francis, who naturally made his way over to the drinks tray.

'Francis, Chief Inspector Maigret wishes to ask you a question and I authorize you to answer him.'

This was the second time today that someone was being authorized to speak to him. And it was not only because, as the magistrate had said, he was on holiday. It was a question of caste, in a way, and Maigret was beginning to get hot under the collar.

'Tell me,' he said, in the most direct manner possible, 'where have you put the silver knife?'

He didn't bother to watch the doctor. It was the butler whose face he stared into, and Francis racked his brains and turned to his master.

'Isn't it in its usual place? . . . I swear to you I haven't taken it . . . With your permission, I'll go and look . . .'

So the silver knife did not belong to the realm of nightmares. It was there in the house, the same knife that had haunted the delirium of Lili Godreau at the hospital.

'There's no need,' said Maigret brusquely. 'Thank you very much.'

'Is that all?'

Before exiting, Francis couldn't help darting him a reproachful look. Hadn't they been friends, the previous evening, in La Popine's dining room? Hadn't he told Maigret everything he knew? Why now was he as good as calling him a thief in front of people?

'I remain at your disposal, Monsieur Maigret,' said Bellamy.

'And I would not wish to abuse your patience, nor that of Monsieur de Folletier.'

The latter took his watch from his pocket as if to say that, indeed, this was beginning to drag on. That Maigret should come and put on his little act in the study where the two friends were chatting was one thing, but now he was making himself too much at home, like children who are brought in to be introduced to the grown-ups and who take advantage to misbehave.

'I wish, doctor, to have a look at your consulting room.'

'Your wish is my command.'

Was there not a certain weariness in his voice?

'You can follow us, Alain. I don't believe you've ever had the opportunity to visit the annexe.'

They went downstairs, Maigret in front, the other two men behind, and the magistrate spoke to his friend in hushed tones. They went through a door into the garden, which they crossed, skirting a little ornamental fountain.

At the bottom of the garden was a red-brick garage which must have looked on to the little sidestreet and, next to the garage, a two-storey building, whose door the doctor opened with a key which he took from his pocket.

The corridor was cold and bare; the waiting room, which Maigret only glimpsed, ordinary. At least the chairs weren't threadbare, as they are in most doctors' waiting rooms, and there weren't the usual watercolours on the walls. However, there was a pedestal table with the customary pile of magazines and picture stories.

'If you would like to follow me . . .'

At the top of the stairs, there were only two rooms. The

largest, very light and airy, was the consulting room. It was comfortably furnished. On either side of the desk, which was as vast as the one in the study, were two good leather armchairs. Against a wall, a narrow divan, not at all sagging and also upholstered in leather, must have served as the examining couch.

The panes of the two windows that looked on to the garden were of frosted glass and received the sun directly in the afternoon. The ones that overlooked the street had curtains: there was no view, only the blind wall of a warehouse.

Maigret opened the door into the adjacent room a fraction. It was narrower and contained a wash-basin and glass-fronted cabinets where nickel instruments were carefully laid out.

He looked slowly about him, his hands in his pockets, much to the annoyance of the magistrate, who was becoming increasingly vexed by his attitude. Then he leaned over the desk.

'The silver knife isn't in its place,' he stated simply.

'Who told you that this is its place?'

'I am merely making an assumption. If you would like to call your butler, it is easy to ask him the question.'

'There was indeed a silver-handled paper knife on my desk. I hadn't even noticed it had gone . . .'

'But you have seen patients here since the 1st of August?'

'Generally I see patients three times a week and sometimes, on other days, by appointment.'

'What are your surgery hours?'

'They're on the copper plate outside. Monday, Wednesday and Friday mornings, between ten and twelve.'

'Never in the evening?'

'Pardon?'

'I am asking you if you ever see patients in the evening.'

'Rarely. Very occasionally, should the occasion arise that a patient is unable to come during the day.'

'Has the occasion arisen recently?'

'I don't recall, but I give you permission to look at the counterfoils in my receipt book.'

Maigret flicked through it shamelessly, and read names that meant nothing to him.

'Would anyone from the house allow themselves to disturb you when you are here?'

'What do you mean by "anyone from the house"?'

'A servant, for example . . . your butler . . . or Madame Bellamy's maid . . .'

'Most certainly not. There is an intercom connecting the annexe to the main house.'

'Your wife?'

'I don't think she has ever set foot inside this consulting room. Perhaps, when I married her and I showed her around the house.'

'Your mother?'

'She only comes when I'm not here, when the place is being spring-cleaned, to keep an eye on the servants.'

'Your sister-in-law?'

'No.'

The two men no longer troubled with formalities. Their exchanges were short and sharp. Neither attempted to look at the other with civility.

Maigret, completely relaxed, opened one of the windows and they could see the trees in the garden. Between a beech and a darker green pine tree, part of the house was visible, particularly two first-floor windows and a skylight on the second floor which was under the eaves.

'Those windows belong to which bedrooms?'

'The one on the left is a corridor, and the one on the right is my sister-in-law's bathroom.'

'And the one above?'

'It's Jeanne's – I mean, the maid's room.'

'And you don't know which day the knife disappeared?'

'I wasn't even aware of it until you came here. Here in my consulting room I don't often need to cut the pages of a book. As for the post, it is delivered to the house and I usually open it in my study.'

'Thank you very much . . .'

'Is that all?'

'That is all. I'll leave by the street door, if you don't mind.'

On the stairs, he turned round.

'By the way, what time did you come home last night?'

'I can't tell you precisely, but it must have been around midnight. Francis had gone home but had left the whisky tray in the study. I came down to get some ice from the refrigerator.'

'And did you see your wife?'

'No.'

'Has her mother visited her?'

'This morning, before the funeral.'

'In your presence?'

'Yes.'

He remained unruffled. The machine was operating admirably, without a hiccup, without any hesitation. Only his voice was slightly more nervous, more trenchant.

The previous day, they had been two companionable men who were getting to know one another. Today, they were at loggerheads.

'Do you still authorize me to come and see you, doctor? Mind you, as Monsieur Alain de Folletier so accurately put it, I am here on holiday and am not entitled to ask anything of you. He himself, even though he is an examining magistrate and is at Les Sables d'Olonne on official business, is only at your house as a friend . . .'

'I remain at your disposal.'

He had removed the chain from the door, and released the latch.

'See you soon, doctor.'

'Whenever you like.'

There was a moment's hesitation as Maigret stepped through the doorway, then the doctor held out his hand and Maigret shook it. It was the magistrate who pretended not to see the hand that Maigret proffered in turn.

'Good night, Monsieur de Folletier. I'd like to mention to you just in case, for the purposes of your investigation, that yesterday, at around four in the afternoon, little Lucile Duffieux came out of Madame Bellamy's bedroom.'

'I know.'

Maigret, who was already in the street, was taken aback, and wheeled round.

'My friend Philippe told me about it well before you arrived, inspector. Good night!'

There was no one in the back street, where there was nothing but bare walls, the locked door of the doctor's garage and the small whitewashed building with its waiting room on the ground floor and consulting room upstairs.

A brass plate engraved with Doctor Bellamy's name stated his consulting days and times. Another little plate requested patients to press the bell and enter.

7.

The street on the outer limits of the town had returned to normal. Occasionally there was an old man sitting outside his house, smoking a pipe. Occasionally too, through an open door, a strident voice could be heard calling a child. Kids played ball in the middle of the road, while somewhere a toddler, all alone, wearing nothing but a blue shirt, dragged his bare buttocks over the uncobbled pavement.

The bereaved family's door was closed. At last they were being left in peace, and it was Maigret who had to disturb them once again. The examining magistrate's words had filled him with amazement. So it was Doctor Bellamy who had been the first to talk to him about the girl's visit to his house the previous day.

On reflection, it made sense for him to take the initiative, since Maigret had seen the girl. What explanation could he give for her presence in his wife's room?

Maigret knocked. He heard the sound of a chair scraping the tiled floor of the kitchen and the door opened; standing before him was the fat woman from that morning. Maybe she recognized him? Maybe, having had to open the door to so many people during the day, she had said to herself that one more or one less made no difference.

One finger on her lips, she said:

'Shhh . . . She's asleep . . .'

Maigret went in, removed his hat and looked at the door to the bedroom, which had been left ajar so as to hear the slightest sound from Madame Duffieux, whom the doctor had sedated.

Why did Maigret feel a wintry chill, as he had done that morning, when they were in the middle of August? Perhaps it is always like that in these little houses. It was already dark inside, as if it were dusk. The stove was lit and a pot of soup was simmering away, giving off an aroma of leeks. It was probably the humming gas ring with its small red disc that reminded him of winter.

Duffieux, his shirt open at the neck, was sitting in a wicker chair, his head lolling back, his mouth half open. He too was asleep, with an expression of bewilderment and despair still etched on his face.

How had the old woman managed to tidy the place up and wash everything after the comings and goings of the police? The house smelled clean, of soap. Sitting down, the woman mechanically picked up her knitting, for women like her are never idle.

Maigret drew up a chair and sat in front of the stove. He knew that for some people, the stove is company. He asked quietly:

'Are you a member of the family?'

'The children call me aunty,' she replied while continuing to count her stitches. 'But I'm not a relative. I live three doors down. I was the one who came when Marthe gave birth. I used to mind the little one for her when she did her errands. She's never been in good health.'

'Has anyone found out why Lucile went to Doctor Bellamy's house yesterday?'

'She went to the doctor's house? . . . They didn't tell me . . . Weren't you with them? . . . Hold on . . . They told me about the money they found in the tin, and the raffle tickets . . . That must be it . . . Go into the bedroom . . . My old legs are too tired . . . Open the wardrobe . . . After they left, I put everything back in its place more or less . . . At the back on the right, you'll find a tin . . .'

The body had been removed. Like Lili Godreau, little Lucile was to be subjected to the ultimate ravages of an autopsy.

Maigret followed the old woman's instructions. Under the clothes, which the inspectors must have examined from every angle, he found an old biscuit tin, which he took into the kitchen.

The woman watched him open the lid and count the bank notes and small change. Was it the tinkle of the coins? Duffieux half-opened his eyes and, seeing another stranger's face in his house, decided to close them again and try to go back to sleep.

The tin contained two hundred and thirty-five francs. There were also raffle tickets in aid of the schools' fund, in booklets of tickets with stubs. Each ticket cost one franc, or twenty five francs for the entire booklet.

Most of the tickets had been sold singly and the stubs bore the names of neighbours. On a sheet of paper torn out of a school exercise book, the girl had written in pencil:

Malterre: 1 book
Jongen: 1 book
Mathis: 1 book
Bellamy: 1 book.

The first three names were those of shopkeepers in the town centre.

Once again, the doctor had an explanation that was disarming in its simplicity. All he had needed to say to the magistrate – who, incidentally, had not asked – was:

'Actually, my wife told me that this girl came to see her yesterday afternoon to sell her raffle tickets . . .'

That was not a sufficient explanation for Maigret, because he knew that Madame Bellamy had been expecting the girl. He also knew that she had been to the house before, and that on that occasion she had told Francis her name.

He replaced the money and the booklets, and took the tin back to the wardrobe.

'Do you know the name of her school teacher, madame?'

'Madame Jadin . . . She lives near the cemetery, in a new house. You'll easily recognize it by its yellow façade . . . The gentlemen copied the names that you read in the tin . . . They must have gone to see Madame Jadin too . . .'

'Did they mention Émile to you?'

'So you're not working with them?'

He dodged the question.

'I'm not from the same department.'

'They asked me where the boy was and, when I told them he must be in Paris, they wanted his address. I showed them the postcard . . .'

'And the letter?'

'They didn't talk about it.'

'Would you show it to me?'

'Take it . . . It's in the right-hand drawer of the dresser . . .'

Gérard Duffieux, in his half-sleep, must have heard their conversation like a vague and distant noise. From time to time, he fidgeted a little, but he was too weary to want to wake up fully.

The right-hand drawer was the household's safe. It was full of old letters, bills, photographs, a fat, worn portfolio that contained official documents, Duffieux's military record, the couple's wedding certificate and the children's birth certificates.

'The letter is right on top,' said the woman.

A musky smell rose from the drawer to which mementos of Lucile and her death certificate had been added.

'May I read it?'

And she replied, with a glance at the sleeping man:

'Considering what they've gone through, it won't make much difference, will it?'

The letter was written on headed notepaper from Larue & Georget, the town printers. Each morning, Maigret walked past their workshop and offices on his way from the promenade to the port.

Dearest Mother . . .

The handwriting was firm, close and precise.

You cannot imagine how much, even at the last minute, the idea of the pain I am about to cause you makes me lose heart. Please read this letter slowly, calmly, alone in front of the fire, in your usual chair. I can picture you so clearly! I know that you will cry and that you will have to take off your glasses to wipe them.

All the same, Mother, this is something that happens to all parents. I've thought long and hard about it. I've read many books and I have come to believe that it is one of the laws of nature.

I am not a monster. I am no more selfish than anyone else. Nor am I heartless.

But you see, dear Mother, I have such a need to live. Can you understand that, you who have spent your life making sacrifices for others, for your husband, your children, for anyone who needed you?

I need to live and it's partly your fault. It was you who gave me my early ambitions by depriving yourself to provide me with a good education. Instead of apprenticing me, like other boys of our social class, you wanted me to study and you were proud when I won all the school prizes.

Now, it is too late to turn back the clock. I am suffocating in our little town where there is no future for a boy like me.

When I started working at Larue & Georget, you thought that my livelihood was guaranteed and it pained me to see you so happy.

'You're all set now,' you said.

But you see, I was already dreaming of a different life. When I was allowed to write short articles for the paper, you proudly showed them to the neighbours and when at last a Paris newspaper, whose editor didn't know how young I was, made me the correspondent for Les Sables d'Olonne, you couldn't contain your delight.

You imagined me married in our town. You imagined me buying a little pink house in one of the new neighbourhoods one day.

Thinking about all that is so painful that I am at a loss to find the words to tell you about my decision.

In a few hours, dearest Mother, I shall be gone. I didn't have the courage to talk to you about it, or to tell Father. I think he will understand straight away, because before he lost his arm, he too was ambitious.

Tonight, I am taking the train to Paris. Thanks to my contacts at the newspaper, I have found a modest position that will give me a foot on the ladder. I haven't breathed a word to anyone, not even to my bosses. But don't worry. I am leaving all my affairs in order.

Lucile is the only one who knows, because I needed to confide in someone. She is a good girl and she will do well. She loves you both very much and I hope she will help you gradually to get over my absence.

I wanted at least to give you a big hug before leaving. I did so, and you must have wondered why I clasped you to me for so long.

If we had said goodbye to each other, I would no longer have had the courage to leave.

I hope that my job will soon enable me to carry on helping you out. Please don't hold it against me if, at first, I don't send you anything.

I have grown up a lot in recent months. You haven't noticed. Parents always see their son as a child, even once he has become a man.

But I have become a man. And tell Father that I shall try to behave like a man. And if one day I hurt you, please know that it will not be through my fault. It will be because life has got the better of me.

I'll write again as soon as I have some news. I'll give you an address where you can write to me. You will receive this letter tomorrow morning and, until then, you won't be worried, because I told you that I would be working all night. I shall post it this evening at the station, just before catching the last train. I already have my ticket.

I am going to try my luck, Mother, as so many others have done before me and do every day. I sometimes heard you say that those who leave in this way are not worth much. Believe me, I promise you they are the best.

Wish me luck despite everything. Say a prayer from time to time for your son, who is following his destiny.

Let Father sleep before telling him the news. I know that you are weaker than he is and that you have always been unwell, but over the past few months I have been suspecting that he might have heart disease and has been keeping it from us.

You still have Lucile.

Give her a kiss from me. Be happy, the three of you. I shall try to be happy too and, when we see each other again, I should like to hope that you will have reason to be proud of me.

Goodbye, dearest Mother.

Your son Émile

Maigret picked up the postcard, which had a picture of Place de la Concorde. There were only a few words on the back, the handwriting shakier.

Arrived safely. You can write to me Poste Restante, Post Office 26, Paris. Love and kisses to all three of you.
   Émile

As far as Maigret could recall, Post Office 26 was the one in Faubourg Saint-Denis, near the Grands Boulevards.

'Has he been sent a telegram?' he asked.

'Only at midday.'

'And he hasn't replied yet?'

'Do you think he's received the telegram already? . . . If he were to come, that would be some comfort . . .'

And she looked, sighing, at the man with the empty sleeve who had sunk back into a deep sleep, his breathing making his greying moustache quiver.

'Are you staying with them tonight?'

'Don't worry. I had my nephew go and pick up my things.'

She wouldn't go to bed, for she wouldn't dare sleep in the room where Lucile had been strangled. She would take care of Madame Duffieux. Would the husband go to work as usual?

He preferred not to ask any questions. Slowly, he folded up the letter, which he put back in the drawer. He would have liked to take it with him, but he knew he would not be allowed to.

In the bedroom Madame Duffieux was beginning to moan like a child and the neighbour struggled to her feet.

'I'm sorry,' mumbled Maigret. 'I had to come—'

She motioned to him to be quiet and, as he left, tiptoed into the grieving woman's room.

There was a piano in a corner, an embroidered runner on the oak table and, on the walls, photographs of children in rows, each one from a different year. Madame Jadin's pupils, year by year.

'One of your colleagues has already come here and questioned me, inspector, a tall one with a scar . . .'

That was Piéchaud, who knew his job.

'There is indeed a raffle held in aid of the schools' fund . . . It's the pupils who sell the tickets . . . We allow them to go around the shopkeepers and people they know in general . . . Our Lucile had tickets like everyone else . . . It was Monday morning that the children were to bring back the unsold tickets and the stubs . . .'

'Was each pupil assigned to a particular neighbourhood or street?'

'They were free—'

'Tell me about Lucile, would you?'

Madame Jadin was short and dark. In class, she must seem strict, because it was required, but there was a lot of kindness in her eyes.

'The questions your inspector asked me made me a little indignant, I confess, and he will probably tell you that I didn't give him a very warm reception. You seem more understanding. He insisted on knowing whether Lucile spent a lot of time with boys, whether she was highly sexually aware or not. To think that she was barely four-

143

teen! She looked older, because she was tall and thoughtful, even a little too thoughtful for her age . . . I don't deny that we do sometimes have girls who are too precocious, who meet boys in the street, especially in winter, when it is dark, and some of them − but they are the exception − go for men . . .'

'Was Lucile a good girl?'

'I used to call her "little mother" because at break, instead of playing with the older children, she preferred to look after the young ones in the nursery class . . . One day, I overheard a conversation between her and one of her friends, who had had a new baby brother. Lucile was saying wistfully: "Well, it seems my mother can't have any more children . . ."'

'There are more girls than one would believe, inspector, especially among the most deprived, who are already fully grown women at fourteen . . .'

'I presume that you hadn't seen her recently because of the school holidays?'

'I saw her several times, because we run summer activities to keep the children off the streets. We organize games, we take them to the beach or into the pine woods . . .'

'Did you find Lucile changed?'

'I noticed that she was worried and I asked her if anything was the matter. I don't know if it is the same in boys' classes, but with girls, we all have our favourites . . . Lucile was my pet . . . At break, during the school term, or in the pine woods during the holidays, she would gladly leave her friends to come and chat with me . . .

'I remember asking her if it was true that her brother had gone away.'

'So that was only a few days ago at most?'

'It was three days ago . . . I heard about it from the other children . . . Instead of answering me honestly, as she usually did, looking straight at me, she looked away and snapped: "Yes."

'"I imagine your mother is very upset?" I asked.

'"I don't know."

'"Has she heard from him?"

'"I don't know."

'I didn't press the matter because I could see she was distraught and tense.

'That is all I can tell you, inspector . . .'

'Do you teach the piano?'

'A few private lessons.'

'Did Lucile take lessons with you?'

Madame Jadin nodded, looking slightly embarrassed, which doubtless meant that the girl's parents couldn't afford such a luxury for their daughter.

When Maigret reached the Larue & Georget printing works in Rue Saint-Charles, the workers were leaving to go home. He crossed the cobbled yard, walked round a lorry, and pushed open a glass door above which was a sign saying 'Office'.

A typist was putting on her hat.

'Is Monsieur Larue here?' he asked.

'Monsieur Larue died two months ago.'

'I'm sorry. In that case, may I speak to Monsieur Georget?'

The latter, who was in an adjacent room, must have heard him, for he said loudly:

'Show the gentleman in, Mademoiselle Berthe.'

He was a short man, rather shabbily dressed, and was busy correcting the galley proofs of his newspaper. The four-page weekly *L'Écho des Sables* contained mainly local news and classified advertisements, particularly legal notices.

'Do sit down, inspector. Don't be surprised that I know who you are. I am an old friend of Chief Inspector Mansuy's, and he told me about you. I see you walking past every morning. I was certain that you would come to see me.'

And, as Maigret anticipated, he added:

'One of your colleagues came earlier, his name was . . . hold on . . .'

'Boivert . . .'

'That's it! Well, I didn't have much to say to him. Is it true that you're conducting your own investigation?'

'Is that what Boivert told you?'

'Not at all! . . . It's a rumour going around town . . . For instance, I was at the funeral this morning – Doctor Bellamy is one of my clients . . . Two people at least told me the same thing . . . They are also saying that you have your own idea, that the Poitiers police don't agree with you and that you have a surprise in store for us—'

'People talk too much,' grumbled Maigret irritably.

'Do you want me to tell you what I know about Émile Duffieux?'

Maigret nodded, but only appeared to be half listening.

'He's the second boy of this type who's passed through my hands. Both of them had some rough edges that needed knocking off, if you see what I mean . . . He's also the second one to slip through my fingers . . . I don't hold it against them, mind you . . . The first one is a journalist in Rennes now, and I read his articles every morning in *L'Ouest-Éclair*. As for Émile . . . we'll see sooner or later what will become of him, won't we?'

'I hope so.'

The ominous tone in which Maigret said those words made Monsieur Georget shudder.

'In any case, inspector, he's an honest boy. His only fault, you could say, is a certain wariness . . . That's not the right word . . . He tends to be withdrawn . . . It's as if he's always afraid of a mocking smile, a rebuff, or simply condescension . . . His family's poverty weighs on him and yet he is not ashamed of it . . . When someone asks what his father does, he's quick to reply "night watchman".

'And he doesn't take the trouble to add that Duffieux only took on the job after having his right arm amputated . . .

'I don't know if I'm making myself clear . . . He wants to succeed at all costs . . . He will work as hard as is necessary to do so . . . He has read tons of books, whatever he can get his hands on . . . His mood swings between anxiety and ebullience . . .'

'Women?' asked Maigret.

The printer jerked his head in the direction of the office.

'Has she gone out?' he asked quietly, meaning the typist. He went next door to be certain.

'As you have seen, Mademoiselle Berthe is pretty, delectable even. All my male employees have tried to woo her. The fact is that she's head over heels in love with Émile Duffieux and defends him fiercely if you say a word against him in front of her. She did everything she could to attract his attention. She became flirtatious, changed her dress two or three times a week. I wonder whether he even noticed. He had set himself a goal. I was always expecting to see him leave for Nantes or Bordeaux, like most of our ambitious youngsters. But he went straight to Paris . . .'

'Did he tell you in person?'

'No, by letter.'

'Which you received the day after his departure?'

'Exactly . . . Like his parents . . . It was as if he was afraid that at the last minute someone would put a spoke in his wheel . . . No need to add that he left everything in good order . . . If you would like to see the letter . . .'

Maigret merely glanced at it. Émile apologized very nicely and, just as nicely, thanked his employer for all he had done for him.

'Did his sister ever come to the office to see him?'

'I don't recall . . . Besides, Duffieux spent little time in the office . . . These past months at least he was very much involved with the newspaper, both the news side and the classified ads, because in a little establishment like ours, you have to turn your hand to everything.'

'I should like to have as precise an idea as possible of his schedule.'

'He would arrive at around nine, sometimes earlier, because he wasn't a clock-watcher . . . And he would generally stay in the office until ten thirty . . . Then he'd drop into the police station for the latest news, then the town hall and the sub-prefecture . . . Sometimes, we would just see him for a few minutes around midday, other times he came back only after lunch. In the afternoon, he would write his articles and go into the workshop to supervise the layout . . . He'd also run a few errands, telephone lawyers, estate agents, the managers of the cinemas whose programmes we print . . .

'That's on a normal day . . . On Fridays, the day the paper is printed, he'd often stay behind with me until nine o'clock at night.'

It was more or less the life of a provincial reporter.

'In short,' Maigret summed up, 'it was mainly in the morning that he was out and about. Do you know whether he received any private telephone calls?'

'That depends what you mean by private. I knew he was the correspondent for a Paris paper. He had asked my permission to accept the job. It took very little of his time because it was the same news as ours that he sent them . . . I gave him permission to use one of our telephone lines and he kept a note of his calls, which the book-keeper deducted from his pay each month. I never caught him making a private call, to a friend, for example . . .'

'Thank you.'

'No one has been able to contact him in Paris yet?'

'He only gave his parents a poste restante address.'

'That can take a day or two, of course . . .'

The printer had just unwittingly given Maigret an idea. The minute he was back at the hotel, he called the Police Judiciaire.

'Hello! . . . Is Lucas there? . . . Who's speaking? . . . Tor-rence? . . . Maigret here . . . Still on holiday, yes . . . What? . . . Is the weather good? . . . I have no idea . . . I'll go and have a look . . . It's not sunny, but it's not raining . . . Is Jan-vier still at his desk? . . . Put him on, would you . . . Yes, thank you . . . Hello, is that you, Janvier? . . . Not too busy? . . . The usual? . . . Right . . . Do you want to run an errand for me? . . . I'd like you to go to Post Office 26 . . . That's the one in Faubourg Saint-Denis, isn't it? . . . Yes, I know . . . Go and see the poste restante clerk and ask him if there are any letters for Émile Duffieux . . . Yes, make a note . . . Émile . . . Duffieux . . . No, double F . . . F for Fernand . . . Hold on! . . . The most important thing is to ask whether anyone has turned up to collect his post . . . Yes . . . And on what date . . . If he hasn't come yet, ask the clerk to telephone you as soon as he does . . . Tell him to waylay his customer for a few minutes somehow and you jump into a taxi . . .

'Above all, no blunders. Simply ask him for his address . . . Follow him if necessary . . .

'Don't hang up yet . . . After that, go down and have a look at the hotel records from the past few days . . . Espe-cially those from the 31st of July and the 1st of August . . . Look for the same name . . .

'That's all . . . No, it's not an important case . . . A simple errand on a personal matter . . .

'Thank you, my friend . . . That's right . . . She's better, yes . . . Say hello to Marie-France for me . . .'

'The gentlemen from Poitiers are already about to eat,' murmured Monsieur Léonard, who was standing behind Maigret holding a bottle.

'Let them stay where they are.'

'But you'll have a little . . .'

Go on! It would be best to have a little drink so as not to offend the good man.

'I found them two rooms, in different hotels. They aren't very happy. Is it my fault? To your good health . . .'

'To yours, Monsieur Léonard . . .'

'Do you think they'll find the bastard who strangled the girl?'

It was eight o'clock. The lights had been switched on. The two men were sitting in the back room, between the kitchen and the dining room. Behind them, the waitresses were going back and forth carrying trays.

Was it Monsieur Léonard's words that suddenly gave Maigret food for thought? He frowned.

'Are you not eating?'

'Not now . . .'

He was about to go up to his room, and do something he rarely did, and only in particularly serious cases.

He remembered his anguish the previous evening, when he had desperately sought to identify the girl he had encountered on the stairs at the doctor's. The people he had questioned looked at him in amazement, even Mansuy, even the guardroom officers. And yet, if at that point he had been able to find out a name, an address, Lucile would still be alive.

Maybe he was completely wrong. But if he wasn't, then other people were in danger, starting with himself.

That was why he had to go up to his room and put his suspicions down on paper.

'Are you going out?'

'Just for an hour. Save me something to eat . . .'

He would write his report at night, calmly, before going to bed. Now, he headed for the railway station. Hadn't Émile Duffieux, in his letter to his mother, said that he'd bought his ticket in advance?

The ill-lit station was almost deserted. On the tracks, there was only a local train with old-style carriages. The man at the ticket window wore a deputy stationmaster's cap.

'Good evening, inspector . . .'

Too many people recognized him, that was a fact.

'I would like to ask you something. Do you know young Duffieux?'

'Monsieur Émile? . . . Of course I knew him . . . As a reporter, he would come to the station every time an important person was expected . . . I let him on to the platform . . .'

'In that case, perhaps you can tell me whether he came to buy a ticket for Paris at the end of last month?'

'I am well placed to answer you since I was the one who sold them to him.'

Maigret was immediately struck by his use of the plural.

'You sold him several tickets?'

'Two, second class . . .'

'Returns?'

'No, singles . . .'

'Around what time did he come and pick them up?'

'In the morning, just before midday . . . He wanted them for the last train, the 22.52 . . .'

'Do you happen to know whether he took that train?'

'I presume so . . . I'm going to leave the station in a few minutes . . . At that time, it's the deputy night station-master who's on duty . . .'

'Is he here yet?'

'He must be . . . Come into the office . . .'

They went on to the platform and then into an office where the telegraph was whirring and clicking away.

'Hey, Alfred . . . This is Detective Chief Inspector Maigret, you must have heard of him . . .'

'Pleased to meet you . . .'

'He'd like to know whether young Duffieux boarded the 163 on one of the last days of July . . . I sold him two second-class singles for Paris in the morning . . . He was planning to get the 22.52.'

'I don't remember . . .'

'Do you think you'd have seen him if he'd taken that train?'

'I can't swear to it . . . Sometimes, at the last minute, you're called away to the telephone or to the mail compartment . . . I'd be surprised, though, if I hadn't noticed him . . .'

'Is it possible to find out whether the tickets have been used?'

'In theory, yes . . . We'd just have to ask Paris . . . As you know, passengers have to hand in their tickets at the exit . . . but some of them get off before Paris . . . Others get swept along by the crowd and forget to hand in their ticket . . . It's rare . . . It's against the rules . . . You're supposed to . . .'

He pondered for a moment, and murmured:

'There's something odd . . .'

He looked at his colleague, as if he too should be struck by something that wasn't right.

'Émile Duffieux took the train several times, to Nantes, to La Roche or to La Rochelle . . . Each time he had a free pass . . .'

He explained to Maigret:

'Journalists are entitled to travel free in first class. They simply have to request a pass from their newspaper. It would have been particularly worth his while this time, since it was a long journey . . . I wonder why he bought second-class tickets when he could have travelled first class free of charge . . .'

'He wasn't alone,' Maigret pointed out.

'Of course . . . It was probably a woman. But you know, even in such cases, these gentlemen from the press blithely take advantage . . .'

Maigret found himself in the street, and a little later walked past La Popine's shop. The shutters were closed and there was a light beneath the door. It was much too early. Francis must be busy serving dinner at the doctor's house.

He continued down narrow, dingy streets, shivering occasionally on hearing footsteps behind him.

If he was right, if events had taken place as he had gradually pieced them together, although there were some gaps, shouldn't they expect further victims — at least one — in addition to Lili Godreau and little Lucile?

He suddenly swung round and went into the Hôtel de Vendée.

'Is Madame Godreau still here?' he asked the owner, who sat at the counter herself, wearing black silk and a large cameo brooch.

'You are forgetting, inspector . . .'

He was furious at being recognized wherever he went.

'You are forgetting that her name is no longer Madame Godreau, but Madame Esteva . . . She and Monsieur Esteva left on the 5.30 train.'

'I presume,' he added tetchily, for he knew the reply already, 'that her son-in-law came to see her yesterday evening?'

'That's correct . . . They were in fact the last to leave the little parlour . . .'

'Was Monsieur Esteva with them?'

'I think, but I can't be sure, that Monsieur Esteva was the first to go upstairs.'

'Thank you very much.'

He had spent the entire day saying 'Thank you very much'.

One person at least was in danger, or else he was completely mistaken.

And, unfortunately, about that person, he knew nothing, not even whether it was a man or a woman, and he could guess neither their age nor their profession.

All he knew was that they were in the town, in the centre of town most likely, within a radius that he could almost have drawn on a map.

There was no way he could deal with it that evening. He would have to wait until daylight, when the shops and cafés were open.

Then the hunt would be on, the only vital lead being his conviction, and he would have to keep repeating his never-ending thank-yous.

Providing there was still time!

The two inspectors had finished dinner and were smoking cigarettes and drinking brandy when Maigret sat down at the table in the almost empty dining room.

'Well, chief?'

And he, surlier than ever, an unpleasant taste of tiredness in his mouth, like after a long train journey, grunted:

'Well, nothing, dammit!'

8.

At eleven o'clock the next morning, Maigret pushed open a door, perhaps the hundredth, and this time it was a leather goods shop. He had started at one end of the town at eight o'clock, when the bigger and more elegant establishments are still closed. He entered shops that only the women in the neighbourhood went to. Anyone observing from the outside would see him, too tall and too broad, scraping his head on the brooms and mops hanging from the ceiling, looking around sullenly, waiting his turn, surrounded by bareheaded housewives. They would also note that after the fourth or fifth shop, it was clear that his lips formed the same words each time.

With the difference that, initially, he had felt obliged to buy something. In the cafés, it was easy: he would drink a glass of white wine. In a grocer's, he had bought a small packet of pepper, because at that point he thought that he would have a lot of other shops to visit and he couldn't saddle himself with bulky items.

In a haberdasher's with grimy windows, where he had bought a reel of cotton, an elderly spinster sprouting hairs on her chin and exuding a strong, musty smell had given him a funny look.

'Do you know Madame Bellamy?' recited Maigret.

'The mother or the wife?'

'The wife.'

'I know her and everyone else.'

'Do you sometimes see her walk past in the street?'

These were the ritual questions he tirelessly asked.

'Now look here, monsieur. I have enough work not to poke my nose into what's going on in the street. If I have a piece of advice for you, it's to do the same.'

When people thought he meant Madame Bellamy the mother, their faces generally became hostile. La Popine was right: the elderly lady with a walking stick inspired little affection among the town's shopkeepers.

So to keep things simple, he had learned to say:

'Do you know Doctor Bellamy's wife?'

And he had stopped making purchases. Either people already knew him by sight, or they assumed he was a police officer.

He had started out in the northern part of town, in other words, in the port district, combing the streets that Madame Bellamy could have taken to go to the fish market, for example.

'Of course I know her. I often used to see her. She's a very beautiful woman. I still see her drive past in the car, with her husband—'

'But you don't see her out and about?'

Husbands turned to their wives, or wives to their husbands.

'What about you, do you ever see her walking past?'

They shook their heads. Odette Bellamy did not come to this neighbourhood, or that of Notre-Dame, or the town centre.

'Excuse me, madame, do you know Doctor Bellamy's wife?'

He did not only ask the shopkeepers. He asked women in their doorways and even an elderly cripple who must spend his days sitting at his open window.

It was a painstaking, repugnant task, which made him feel slightly ashamed. He could imagine the comments being made behind his back.

At ten o'clock, he had covered most of the arc of the circle around the doctor's house. If Odette Bellamy ever went out alone, on foot, it was now certain that she could only follow Le Remblai.

He returned there. Most of the shops were expensive-looking.

'Excuse me, madame, do you know . . .'

And now, at last, his efforts were rewarded. It began with the cake shop almost next door to the big white house.

'She hasn't gone out much since her marriage. But I do sometimes see her in the morning . . .'

This round, rosy-cheeked woman could not suspect how much joy she brought to Maigret's heart.

'Perhaps to walk her dog?'

'Does she have a dog? I've never seen it. I'd be surprised if there were a dog in the doctor's house.'

'Why is that?'

'I don't know. He doesn't seem to me to be the type to have a dog. No! I suppose she goes out shopping. She usually wears a little suit. She tends to walk briskly . . .'

'Around what time does she go past?'

'Oh! It's not every day, you know. I can't even say that it's often . . . If I notice her, it's because it's almost always at the time I'm putting the cakes in the window . . . Around ten o'clock . . . I sometimes see her coming back . . .'

'Much later?'

'Perhaps an hour afterwards? . . . I couldn't swear to it . . . you know, so many people go past . . .'

'Do you see her several times a month?'

'I don't know . . . I don't want to mislead you . . . Let's say once a week, for instance . . . Sometimes twice . . .'

'Thank you *very* much . . .'

He had been repeating those four words ad nauseam all morning, even to the bearded haberdasher woman who had put him in his place.

And, since the cake shop, he had stayed on the trail. Sometimes it was a long and tedious process. It took patience to jog people's memories.

'In which direction does she walk?'

'Towards the end of Le Remblai.'

'In the direction of the pier or the pine woods?'

'The pines.'

There were gaps. If a street ran into the promenade at that point, he had to check it out to make sure that Madame Bellamy didn't take it.

The two inspectors, Piéchaud and Boivert, who had enjoyed a lie-in, walked past him, fresh and rosy-cheeked. They saw him go into a hair salon and must have thought that he was going to have a haircut. From a distance, Maigret could clearly see the windows of the white house.

Why did he have the feeling he was being watched?

Today was Friday. It was the doctor's consulting day: from ten to twelve, he should have been in the annexe at the bottom of the garden.

But there was nothing stopping him from leaving his patients in the lurch or getting rid of them quickly to go and stand behind the louvred shutters of the library. With binoculars it was the ideal place to follow Maigret's comings and goings.

Was Bellamy watching him?

'Either I'm wrong or . . .'

The same words had been going round and round in Maigret's head since the previous evening and he remained conscious of a threat, not so much to himself – not immediately – but to some unknown person. He was so concerned that in the morning, he had telephoned Chief Inspector Mansuy, not without some trepidation.

'Maigret here . . . Tell me, do you have anything to report? . . . No violent deaths? . . . No missing persons? . . .'

Mansuy had thought he was joking.

'I'd like to ask you a personal favour. You know the municipal departments better than I do . . .'

Each time he telephoned from the Hôtel Bel Air, hc could be certain that Monsieur Léonard was not far away, watching him like a faithful dog.

'Émile Duffieux was in the habit of dropping in to your station every morning, then calling into the town hall and finally the sub-prefecture, to gather news . . . What? It's your secretary he used to see? . . . It doesn't matter

. . . Try to understand my question . . . In theory, he should have been with you at around ten fifteen, ten thirty at the latest. That enables you to work out what time he arrived, still in theory, at the town hall and at the sub-prefecture . . .'

'I can tell you straight away . . .'

'Hold on . . . you haven't understood what I'm getting at . . . I said, and I repeat, *in theory* . . . What I need to know is whether his hours were regular . . . If for example, from time to time, on a specific day or otherwise, he did his round a lot later . . .'

'Understood . . .'

'I'll telephone you for your answer, or I'll come and see you later on.'

'Do you have any news?'

'Nothing.'

The telephone call Maigret had received from Janvier late in the evening could hardly be called news. Émile Duffieux had not yet turned up at the poste restante. There were three letters for him, all postmarked Les Sables d'Olonne. Two were in the same handwriting.

'A girl's writing,' added Janvier. 'Should I take them and send them to you?'

'Leave them at the post office until further orders.'

'There's also a telegram.'

'I know. Thank you.'

The telegram informing the young man of his sister's death.

As he hung up, Maigret was on the point of giving the inspector a new task but he felt that he alone was the person who could accomplish it successfully. He couldn't be in Les Sables d'Olonne and Paris at the same time. Was he right to opt for Les Sables d'Olonne, for this dubious, painstaking chore that he had been carrying out since first light?

'Odette Bellamy? . . . But of course, inspector . . .'

The fine leather goods dealer was another one who recognized him and spoke to him with the familiarity of a fan talking about a favourite film star.

'Germaine,' he yelled, 'it's Chief Inspector Maigret . . .'

They were a young, pleasant couple.

'Do you have a lead? Is it true what people are saying?'

'I have no idea what people are saying.'

'That you want to arrest an important figure in town and that the examining magistrate is trying to stop you.'

So a tiny grain of truth had found its way into the most outlandish rumours.

'That is false, madame, don't worry. I don't want to arrest anyone.'

'Not even the killer of the Duffieux girl?'

'My colleagues are handling that. I merely wish to ask you a question. Do you know Doctor Bellamy's wife?'

'I know Odette very well.'

'Are you friends?'

'We were, especially before she got married. Since then, we haven't seen much of her.'

'A propos, I'd like to know whether you see her walking past on Le Remblai from time to time?'

'Fairly often.'

'What do you call fairly often?'

'I don't know . . . Once or twice a week? . . . I sometimes talk to her, when I'm standing in the doorway . . .'

'And do you know where she's off to?'

The woman was stunned, like a person who had been expecting a tough test and who is asked the most mundane question.

'Of course!'

'Far from here?'

'Right here . . . The house next door . . .'

'Do you know why she goes there?'

'It's not hard to guess . . . It's obvious you're not a woman, inspector . . . On the first floor of the house next door there's a dressmaker and lingerie shop run by another of my friends, Olga . . . Olga dresses all the most elegant women in Les Sables d'Olonne, except those who go to Nantes or Paris . . . But they too always have little things, even if it's only underwear, that they need making . . .'

'Are you certain that Odette Bellamy doesn't go any further?'

'I've seen her go next door countless times . . . Olga will tell you . . .'

'Thank you *very* much . . .'

He was irked. His thinking was correct, because the young woman did indeed go out alone once or twice a week, but he hadn't been able to follow his idea through.

If he had had a family of his own, as a police officer at the station had said to him the other night, he would immediately have thought of the schoolmistresses.

Had he been a woman, he would immediately have thought of the dressmaker.

'May I use your telephone?'

To call Mansuy.

'I think you're right, inspector. I wonder how you guessed . . . Usually, young Duffieux was very regular . . . He would arrive at each of the places within five minutes of the times you mentioned . . . But, from time to time, he would turn up not late, but nearly two hours later . . . I tried to find out if it was a particular day; unfortunately, no one was able to say . . .'

'Thank you *very* much . . .'

It had become a refrain. He thanked people all day long. He thanked the couple again and went next door, a lovely house several storeys high with a huge, light-filled stairwell and big polished oak doors.

On the first floor, the copper plate on the left-hand door read:

OLGA

Haute couture – Fancy goods – Lingerie

Before going inside, he automatically emptied his pipe by banging it against his heel. A dishevelled little woman rushed up to him.

'Can I help you, monsieur?'

'I'd like to speak to Madame Olga.'

'Who sent you?'

'No one sent me.'

'I'll go and see if Mademoiselle is there.'

She did not have to go far, only through a curtain, from behind which came an exchange of whispers. Then a tall, slim woman came into the pearl-grey waiting room where Maigret stood expectantly.

'Monsieur!'

'Maigret . . . It doesn't matter . . . Mademoiselle Olga?'

'Yes.'

She had a confident step, and her face had sharp, strong features. She was extremely well dressed, in a light suit that made her look like a businesswoman.

'If you would like to come this way into my office . . .'

It was tiny, and smelled of oregano and Virginia tobacco. She held out a cigarette case and he almost took one without realizing.

'One of your customers is Doctor Bellamy's wife, I believe?'

'That is correct. Odette is not just a customer any more, she's a friend.'

'I know.'

'Oh!'

'She comes to see you often, two or three times a week, on average?'

'Possibly. But may I ask . . .?'

'I'm the one who is asking the questions, if you don't mind. Did Doctor Bellamy telephone you this morning by any chance?'

'No. Why?'

'Nor yesterday?'

'Nor yesterday.'

'And he didn't come and see you?'

'He never sets foot here.'

'And you didn't spot him in the street? Forgive me for pressing the matter. It is of the utmost importance.'

'No . . . I don't see . . .'

'Do you live in this apartment?'

'Not strictly speaking . . . I have two connecting apartments . . . This one comprises only the fitting rooms and the workshop . . . The smaller one, which looks out over the back of the building, is where I live . . .'

'Is there an entrance that isn't on Le Remblai?'

'Like the neighbouring houses, this one has two entrances, one on Le Remblai and the other in Rue du Minage.'

'Listen, Mademoiselle Olga . . .'

'It seems to me that I've done nothing but listen and answer you for a good while.'

She did not lose her cool, but smoked her cigarette and looked him directly in the eyes.

'I've been searching for you since yesterday afternoon.'

She smiled.

'You see, it's not difficult to find me.'

'I need you to answer me truthfully. Make sure no one can hear us.'

He was so insistent that she did as he asked, raised a curtain and went and gave orders to ensure that her staff were out of earshot.

'Your friend Odette did not come here just to see her dressmaker.'

'Do you think?'

Her lip had begun to tremble slightly.

'Time is short. I assure you this is not the moment to try and be clever. Presumably you know who I am?'

'No, but I imagine you're a member of the police force.'

'Detective Chief Inspector Maigret . . .'

'Pleased to meet you.'

'I am here on holiday. I am not in charge of any investigation. Two tragedies at least have occurred within a few days without my being able to avert them. If everyone had been truthful with me, I could have prevented the second.'

'I don't see what . . .'

'Yes you do.'

Blood rushed to the young woman's cheeks.

'I wasn't certain I'd find you alive this morning. The Duffieux girl, who knew less than you, was killed the other night.'

'Do you think there's a connection?'

She was beginning to yield. The hardest part of the job was done. She had barely realized what was happening to her, and now there was no going back.

'Did Émile come in via Rue du Minage?'

One last time she opened her mouth to lie or to protest, but there was such determination in the big masculine head coming close to her that she stammered:

'Yes . . .'

'And I suppose that your friend Odette didn't linger in the fitting rooms but went straight to your apartment?'

'How can you know that?'

'Where is she right now?'

'You should know that too.'

'Answer me.'

'But . . . I presume she's in Paris . . .'

Without thinking, Maigret took his pipe out of his pocket and dipped the bowl in his tobacco pouch.

'No,' he said harshly.

'So he didn't leave either?'

'He is no longer in Les Sables d'Olonne.'

'And are you certain that Odette still is? Have you seen her?'

'I haven't seen her with my own eyes, but Doctor Bourgeois, who is treating her, saw her three days ago.'

'I don't understand.'

'That doesn't matter.'

'What about her husband?'

'Exactly!'

'Do you mean he knows?'

'It is more than likely.'

'But then . . . but . . .'

She drew herself up, panic-stricken, and began to pace up and down the little office.

'You have no idea what that means . . .'

'Oh yes I do.'

'He's capable of anything . . . You don't know him as well as I do . . . You don't know his way of loving her . . . You've seen him . . . He seems like a cold man . . . That doesn't stop him throwing himself at Odette's feet sometimes and sobbing like a child . . . If such a thing were possible, he would have locked her away so that no man could lay eyes on her . . .'

'I know.'

'Odette has always been fond of him, and grateful to

him . . . But she wasn't happy . . . A number of times she thought of leaving, and she only stayed for fear of driving him to despair . . .'

'But she did decide to in the end,' muttered Maigret.

'Because she fell in love . . . A man cannot understand these things . . . You probably never met Émile . . . If you'd seen him . . . If you'd seen his eyes, the way his hands shook . . . If you'd felt the passion that . . .'

She stopped, embarrassed.

'Forgive me,' she said calmly. 'That is not what you wanted to know.'

'On the contrary.'

'Well, they were in love, and that's it.'

'That's it, as you say! And Odette asked you to help her meet her young lover.'

'I wouldn't have done it for anyone else.'

'I have no difficulty believing you.'

'I took a huge risk.'

'You did.'

'If there had been a scandal . . .'

'And there will be.'

'So what do you want of me? Why are you trying to alarm me?'

'I am more alarmed than you are. I am trying to piece together the whole story precisely to avert a further tragedy.'

'Are you certain that Odette hasn't left?'

'Yes.'

'I can't believe he left without her.'

'Nor can I.'

She stared at him.

'So what does that mean?'

'He hasn't been seen in Les Sables d'Olonne since the evening set for their elopement. He wasn't seen at the station either. Tell me where they had arranged to meet.'

'In the little street behind the doctor's house.'

'At what time?'

'Around nine thirty.'

'That's the time that Bellamy is usually in the library, close to his wife's bedroom.'

'That evening there was a dinner at the prefecture and he had promised to attend.'

'Are you certain that Odette hasn't telephoned you or given any sign of life since?'

'I swear it, inspector. You will agree that I've been honest with you . . .'

'Do you know where your friend and Émile first met?'

Again she looked flustered.

'I wonder whether I should tell you. You won't understand. It's so childish!'

'I was a child once too.'

'And did you ever spend weeks watching out for a woman and following her in the street? . . . That's what he did . . . When she left her house to come and see me . . . It was last autumn . . . She had to have her entire winter wardrobe made . . . She came more often . . . She chose the time when her husband was seeing patients to feel free, even though at that point she wasn't doing anything wrong . . . Émile followed her . . . You see how easy it is . . .'

'I suppose he started by writing to her?'

'Yes. She didn't reply for over two months. When she did, it was to tell him to leave her alone.'

'I have experienced that.'

'It sounds ridiculous, when it happens to other people.'

But it hadn't seemed ridiculous to her. On the contrary, she seemed to have been passionately involved in her friend's affair.

'It was after that letter that he had the audacity, one morning, to come up here . . . "I absolutely have to speak with you," he said.

'Odette didn't know what to do . . . I couldn't leave them in the fitting room . . . I pushed them into my office . . .

'After that, they carried on writing to each other . . .'

'You acted as go-between, I presume?'

'Yes. Then . . .'

'I understand.'

'It was very sincere, I promise you.'

'Of course!'

'The proof is that Odette had no qualms in giving up everything. In Paris, she would have had to work, for he had only found a modest position. When I asked her whether she'd be taking her dresses and jewellery, she replied, "No, nothing, I want to start my life all over again."'

'What about Bellamy?'

'What do you mean?'

'Did he not suspect anything? Did you ever see him hanging around your place? One important question: did your friend keep her lover's letters?'

'I'm sure she did.'

She realized what he meant.

'Another thing: are you absolutely certain that no one, other than yourself, knows?'

He understood from her discomfort, that something wasn't right.

'I wonder how it didn't occur to me yesterday,' she said almost to herself, pensive. 'In the early spring, Émile was in bed for a week with tonsillitis. The letters continued arriving in my letterbox. I should add that, as a precaution, he never sent them by post. Once I opened the door early in the morning and saw a girl running away . . .'

'Lucile?'

'His sister, yes.'

'Do you think he told her he was leaving?'

'It's possible. I don't know. I don't know any more. It all seemed so straightforward, so easy, so innocent . . .'

'You see, mademoiselle, there is a man who, for the past few days, has been following the same trail as me, with the advantage that he knows a lot more than I do. But this morning, I ended up here . . .'

'How?'

'By going from door to door. Because I took Odette and Émile as my starting point. Because they had to meet somewhere. And I didn't think, as any woman in my place would have done, of the dressmaker. Who paid Madame Bellamy's bills?'

'Her husband sent me a cheque at the end of the year.'

'Does he know that you were childhood friends?'

'I'm sure he does, for Odette and I were constantly together when he fell in love with her.'

'Did she love him?'

'I think so.'

'It was a lukewarm love, wasn't it, in which the big house, the jewellery, the dresses and the car played a large part?'

'It's likely. Odette was always afraid of ending up like her mother. What am I to do now? What are you going to do?'

The telephone rang.

'May I?'

As soon as she picked up the receiver, she turned pale, and gestured to Maigret.

'Yes, doctor . . . Hello, doctor, I can't hear you very well . . . This is Olga, yes . . . Pardon? . . . Could you repeat the name? . . . Maigret? . . .'

She shot Maigret a questioning look and he nodded his head vehemently.

'You want to know if he has been to see me?'

Maigret pointed to the room, and she wasn't sure she understood. She replied on the off chance:

'He is here at the moment . . . No . . . Not long ago . . . Hold on, I think he wants to talk to you.'

Maigret snatched the receiver.

'Hello! . . . Is that you, doctor?'

Silence on the other end of the line.

'I was just about to phone you to request an interview . . . Don't forget that you told me that you would remain at my disposal . . . Hello . . .'

'I'm here, yes.'

'Are you at home at the moment?'

'Yes.'

'With your permission, I'll be there in a few minutes . . . The time it takes to walk half the length of Le Remblai . . . Hello! . . .'

Silence again.

'Can you hear me, doctor?'

'Yes.'

'I am speaking to you as a fellow human being. Hello! . . . I'm pleading with you, I beg you, I command you not to do anything before I get there . . . Hello! . . .'

'Yes . . .'

'You promise?'

Silence.

'Hello! . . . Hello! Mademoiselle . . . Don't cut us off . . . What? . . . He has hung up? . . .'

He hurriedly put on his hat, dashed out of the door and hurtled down the stairs. Almost outside the door, he saw the convertible car belonging to the leather goods shop owner next door and the latter, his hat on his head, came out of his shop and said a few words to his wife.

'Would you drive me to Doctor Bellamy's, please?'

'With pleasure.'

It was only three hundred metres away, but it seemed to Maigret that during the short time it took to get there, he was no longer breathing. His companion looked at him in surprise, so overawed that he didn't dare ask any questions.

He braked hard.

'Shall I wait for you?'

'No thank you . . .'

He rang the electric bell. He pressed the button for a long time. Through the door he heard a woman's voice, that of Doctor Bellamy's mother, saying:

'Francis, go and see who that lout is . . .'

Francis opened the door, stunned to find himself face to face with Maigret in such a state of agitation.

'Is he upstairs?'

'In the library, yes . . . In any case, he was fifteen minutes ago . . .'

Madame Bellamy senior, her walking stick in her hand, appeared in the doorway to one of the drawing rooms, but he didn't bother to greet her. He raced up the stairs. He paused outside Odette's room for a moment. He heard a noise in the corridor. Perhaps otherwise he might have tried to open the door.

Philippe Bellamy was waiting for him, standing stiffly, as in a portrait, with the library's lavishly bound books behind him.

'What are you afraid of?' he asked, as Maigret got his breath back.

A cold irony made his lip curl.

He stepped aside and indicated the room where, the previous evening, the three of them had sat talking, and motioned to his visitor to sit in one of the armchairs.

'You see that I waited for you.'

Why could Maigret not take his eyes off his white hands, as if he were looking for bloodstains?

That gaze too, the doctor understood.

'You do not believe me?'

A hesitation. A moment's thought. Bellamy must be

horrendously tense. He wiped his hand across his fore-head.

'Come.'

He preceded him in the corridor, taking a small key out of his pocket as he walked. Then he stopped outside his wife's door. He turned round and looked at Maigret. Perhaps he was still uncertain?

At last he opened it, slowly, and Maigret saw the gilded atmosphere of the room, whose curtains were drawn.

In a vast silk-padded bed, light-coloured hair was spread over the pillow. A face was visible in half profile, long eyelashes, the curve of a nose with quivering nostrils, the pout of a protruding lip and, on the golden eiderdown, a bare arm lay limply.

Philippe Bellamy stood stock still against the doorpost. And, when Maigret turned towards him, he saw that the doctor's eyes were closed.

'Is she alive?' asked Maigret in a whisper.

'She's alive.'

'Is she asleep?'

'She's asleep.'

Bellamy spoke like a sleepwalker, his eyes still closed, his hands clenched.

'Bourgeois came to see her this morning and gave her a sedative. She must sleep.'

When they were quiet, the young woman's regular breathing could just be heard, as light as the beating of a moth's wings.

Maigret took a step towards the door, then turned round one more time towards the sleeping woman.

The doctor said impatiently:

'Come.'

He carefully locked the door, slipped the key into his pocket and made his way towards the library.

9.

They were ensconced in the library again, Bellamy in his usual chair, at the desk, Maigret in one of the leather armchairs, and they both remained silent. It was not an awkward or hostile silence, but one that afforded a kind of respite.

It was then, after lighting his pipe, that Maigret noticed that a change had come over Bellamy — since the previous day or in the past few minutes? He now looked like a man suffering from a great weariness but who was controlling himself, determined to hold out until the end. There was a thin, deep shadow under his eyes, and his skin was so ashen, so dull, that his mouth seemed red in contrast, as if he were wearing lipstick.

He was conscious of Maigret's unintentional scrutiny, but he did not allow it to trouble him and, when he finally came out of himself, it was to reach for the bell. His gaze, for the first time, seemed to be asking for permission. It cannot be said that he was smiling, and yet his face somehow lit up with something very vague, bitter, a sort of irony towards Maigret, with a hint of self-pity.

Was he thinking, as he pressed the button, that this was perhaps the last time he was acting as a free, wealthy man, in these surroundings that he had so lovingly created?

The way he wiped his hand across his forehead that day

was like a nervous twitch; he did it twice just waiting for Francis to appear.

'Whisky for me,' he said, 'and for you, Monsieur Maigret?'

'Even though it's still early, I'll have something dry, brandy or Armagnac.'

Once the tray was on the table and the drinks poured, the doctor, lit cigarette in hand, said dreamily:

'There are several solutions . . .'

As if it were merely a matter of a problem that they needed to resolve together.

'There is never only one solution,' sighed Maigret, echoing him.

And Maigret rose heavily, and went over to the telephone sitting on the desk.

'May I? . . . Hello! Mademoiselle, put me through to 118 at La Roche-sur-Yon, please . . . Pardon? . . . There's no wait? Hello! . . . I'd like to speak to the examining magistrate Alain de Folletier . . . This is Doctor Bellamy . . . Bellamy, yes . . .

'Hello! . . . Is that you, Judge Folletier? . . . Maigret here. . . Sorry? . . . No, no . . . I am in his office and I'll pass him to you right away . . . I think he wants to ask you to join us without delay . . .'

As if it had been arranged beforehand, he passed the receiver to the doctor, who took it with an air of resignation. Their eyes met for a second. They had understood one another.

'It's me, Alain . . . Yes, I would like you to come and see me as soon as you can get here . . . Pardon? Knowing you, if you start having lunch, you'll be at it for half the after-noon . . . Could you not, just this once, make do with a sandwich and jump into your car? . . . Your wife has taken it to go to Fontenay? . . . In that case, take a taxi . . . Yes . . . we'll wait for you . . . It is quite important . . .'

He hung up and silence reigned again, broken a little later by the ringing of the intercom. Bellamy seemed to be asking for permission to reply, Maigret batted his eyelids.

'Hello! . . . Yes, Mother . . . No . . . I'm going to be busy for quite a while . . . No, no . . . Please have lunch on your own . . . I shan't be coming downstairs . . .'

When he had hung up, he said:

'Admit that you have no proof.'

'That is true.'

There was nothing arrogant about Philippe Bellamy. He was not challenging Maigret. He was simply making a statement, without crowing. They were two men calmly examining the facts.

'I don't know how you intend to proceed with Alain, but given the current state of the investigation, I doubt that you will obtain an arrest warrant. Not only because he is my friend. Any examining magistrate would be reluctant to take on such a responsibility.'

'But,' said Maigret, 'I have to take that responsibility. Do you not think, doctor, that there have been enough victims already?'

Bellamy bowed his head, and it was perhaps to look at his hands.

'Yes,' he finally conceded. 'I thought so before your arrival. For two days, I have been following your reasoning, hour by hour, by watching your actions. This morning, I understood Olga's role before you did, then I saw you going from door to door on Le Remblai and I knew that you'd eventually end up at her place. I was one step ahead of you. While you were going around questioning people, I could have rung the back-door bell—'

'Do you think that would have been sufficient?'

'Mind you, even with Olga's testimony, you have no charge against me. Assumptions perhaps, on which no jury would find a man in my position guilty. What I would like you to understand is that I can still hold my own, play the game, and that I would probably come out of it if not with glory, at least as a free man.'

He gaze seemed to caress his surroundings and once again there was a glimmer of the same irony.

'Only—' he began.

'Only,' Maigret interrupted him, 'you would have to add to the list. And you are beginning to tire of it, aren't you? Even if you hurried, you wouldn't arrive in time. There is something you have forgotten, a person. For the rest you acted alone. But you had to ask for someone's help over one tiny detail.'

Frowning, the doctor racked his brains, as if trying to resolve an equation.

'The picture postcard,' Maigret prompted him. 'The card that had to be posted from Paris without going there. Let me go to Paris tomorrow and summon your mother-in-law to my office at Quai des Orfèvres, let me question her for several hours if necessary . . . Are you with me? She'll talk eventually . . .'

'Maybe.'

'And I must say, it is one of the factors that most surprised me. How did you happen to have a picture postcard of Paris to hand? I went into the bookshop but they didn't have any.'

The doctor shrugged, rose and went over to take something out of a drawer.

'As you can see, I didn't go to the trouble of destroying the others. I must have bought it one day from a beggar or a pedlar. It has been in this drawer for years.'

He held out an envelope that contained around twenty very crude postcards on which was written: 'France's major cities'.

'I wouldn't have thought you capable of imitating a person's handwriting so perfectly.'

'I didn't imitate it.'

Maigret looked up sharply, amazed, admiring.

'You mean . . . ?'

'That he wrote it himself.'

'Dictated by you?'

The doctor shrugged, as if to say that it was too easy. Almost at the same time signalling to Maigret not to move. Then he tiptoed over to the communicating door and flung it open.

The maid was there, all flustered. Bellamy pretended to believe that she had just arrived.

'Did you want to speak to me, Jeanne?'

At last, Maigret caught sight of her. She was a skinny girl, flat-chested and with no hips, and had an unattractive face with irregular features and bad teeth.

'I thought you were having lunch and I came to clean the room.'

'I would rather, Jeanne, that you went to clean my consulting room. Here is the key.'

Once the door had closed, he sighed:

'Now I wouldn't have needed to kill that girl there. Do you understand? I have no idea what she thinks. I don't know how much she has guessed.

'But even if I had killed half the town, even if I were the most heinous monster, you wouldn't get a word out of her.'

A moment ticked by, then the doctor sighed:

'That girl loves me . . .'

Humbly, but passionately, without hope, despite the other love that fired hers.

Jeanne loved him, and the way she jealously surrounded Odette Bellamy with her protective care was another manifestation of that love.

Was the doctor still following Maigret's thinking step by step? In any case, having lit another cigarette and taken a sip of whisky he shook his head.

'You are mistaken. She's not the one . . .'

He took his time before adding, with a quiet melancholy:

'It's my mother! And she loves me too, at least I presume so, since she is as jealous of me as I have ever been of my wife. Doubtless you are wondering how I found out about everything?

'It's both straightforward and silly. In my wife's boudoir, there is a little rosewood Louis XV desk. On it there is a writing case and a blotter. Now no one hates writing more than Odette. I often used to tease her about it and it was I who had to write to our few friends to accept or refuse an invitation.

'But one morning when my wife was in the garden, Mother showed me the blotter. "It looks as if Odette has changed her habits," she simply said.

'For the blotter was covered in traces of ink, as if it had been used to blot a vast number of letters.

'It's simple and silly, you see. One thinks of everything, except little things like that.

'That feels a very long time ago now, whereas it happened only two weeks ago.'

'Did you find the letters?'

'In the hiding place that all women use: under her linen.'

'Did Émile mention their departure?'

'The last letter gave all the details.'

He spoke in a sharp, curt tone.

'It was the day before . . .'

'And you didn't say anything?'

'I didn't give anything away.'

'You were supposed to be going to a dinner at the sub-prefecture, weren't you?'

'A gentlemen's dinner, yes. In evening dress.'

'Did you go?'

'I put in an appearance.'

'After making sure your wife was in no state to go out?'

'That is correct. On the pretext that she seemed on edge – which was true – I gave her some medication which was actually a powerful sedative. Then I put her to bed and locked her in her room.'

'And you went to the meeting place?'

'At the appointed hour, I had returned home. All I needed to do was open the door that you have seen, the one to the waiting room that opens on to the sidestreet. There was a shadow against the wall. The boy was startled. I thought for a moment that he would run off as fast as his legs would carry him and that I would have to give chase.'

'You took him up to your consulting room?'

'Yes. I think I said: "Would you come in for a moment? My wife isn't feeling well and won't be able to leave with you today."'

Maigret imagined the two men in the dark street, Émile holding a suitcase, his two tickets for Paris in his pocket, quaking in his boots.

'Why did you ask him up?'

The doctor looked at him in amazement, as if in asking that question Maigret showed himself not to be his equal.

'I couldn't do that in the street.'

'You had already decided . . .'

The doctor blinked.

'It is very simple, you know. And so much easier than one thinks!'

'Did you have no pity?'

'It didn't occur to me. Still now, the word shocks me.'

'All the same, he loved her.'

'No.'

And the doctor, trembling, stared coldly, straight into Maigret's eyes.

'If you say that, it is because you know nothing. He was

in love, I'll admit. But not in love with her, do you understand? He didn't even know her! He couldn't love her!

'Had he seen her ill, or ugly, had he seen her weak and moaning? Did he cherish her faults, her little weaknesses?

'He didn't know her.

'What he loved was women. Another could have done just as well.

'Do you know what attracted him the most? It was my name, my house, a certain luxury, a certain reputation. It was the dresses she wore and her aura of mystery . . .

'I'll go further, Maigret . . .'

For the first time, he used the familiar 'Maigret'.

'I am certain, you see, that I'm not mistaken. Without me, without my love, he would not have loved her.'

'Did you talk to him for long?'

'Yes. In the situation he was in, *he couldn't refuse to answer me, could he?*'

Now, he looked away, a little ashamed.

'I needed to know,' he confessed quietly. 'All the details, you understand? . . . All the sordid little details . . .'

Up there, in the consulting room, with the frosted-glass windows.

'I needed . . .'

A sort of modesty made Maigret stop him going any further.

'When did you hear a noise?' he asked.

And Bellamy sat up, emerging from his nightmare.

'You know that too, of course. I guessed so yesterday. When you insisted on visiting my consulting room and especially when you opened all the windows.'

'That was the only possible explanation. She *had to have seen* something.'

'Contrary to what I told you on the first day, my sister-in-law loved me. Was it really love? I sometimes wonder whether it wasn't a kind of jealous rage against her sister . . .'

He let his thought hang in the air, and then tried to explain it.

'My mother . . . Jeanne . . . Lili . . . It's a bit as if the women couldn't bear the sight of a certain sort, a certain quality, a certain intensity of love. I was a bachelor for a long time. My friends' wives paid me no particular attention. When I married Odette, there were few who did not appear to be intrigued, then annoyed, then provocative. I never encouraged my sister-in-law. I pretended not to see anything. I would rather not go into details, but I noticed that there was something violently sexual about her feelings for me.'

'Did she spy on you?'

'She must have been curious on seeing the light on in my office. She probably thought I was seeing a woman. She would have been relieved, I think. It would have reinforced her hopes. I don't know how to say this: in her mind it would have given her a hold over me.

'I opened the door, as I did earlier on Jeanne. I've been hearing rustling behind closed doors since I was a child!

'I said the first thing that came into my head, that I was with a patient, and I asked her to go back to the house.'

'Did she see who you were with?'

'I don't know. Perhaps. It is not important.'

'And did you stay with him for a long time?'

'Around a quarter of an hour. He apologized, and promised me he would not try to see Odette again. He spoke of killing himself—'

'And you made him write?'

'Yes.'

'Under what pretext?'

Slight surprise mixed with reproach in Bellamy's eyes, as he grew irritated with Maigret for being obtuse.

'There was no need for a pretext. I think that at first he didn't even know what he was writing.'

'You had brought the postcard with you?'

'Yes.'

'And you were still in dinner dress?'

'Yes.'

'When did you . . .'

'Just as he finished writing. I took the card and put it away.'

Away from the blood!

'I had sat him down in my chair. He still had the penholder in his hand. I was standing behind him and, for a good while, I had been toying with the silver-handled paper knife. It was very simple, Monsieur Maigret. He couldn't live, could he? Especially after the confidences I had pried out of him.'

His lips were barely trembling now, but Maigret was no longer fooled.

'He slumped to the floor. I had planned everything. I had plenty of time. Again, I heard a noise on the other side of the door. I only opened it a fraction. My sister-in-law could just see his feet. "What's going on?" she screamed. "I am ordering you to go back inside the house. My patient has fainted, that's all."

'I don't know whether she believed me. I don't think she entirely believed me, even though my explanation was plausible.

'And you see that I was right, at first, to tell you that you had no charge against me. I defy you to find the body.'

'We always find them in the end,' sighed Maigret.

'I spent part of the night getting rid of it and removing all the traces. I went out to post the letter that I knew was in his pocket, the letter to his parents. He also had one for his employers—'

'And to send the picture postcard to your mother-in-law.'

'That is correct.'

'How did your wife react, the next day, when she woke up from her drugged sleep?'

'I didn't say anything to her. She didn't dare ask me anything.'

'And until now, there has been no discussion of anything between you?'

'No.'

'And you have been in to see her every day?'

'Yes.'

'And you haven't given yourself away?'

'No. She was very weary, very depressed. I ordered her to stay in bed.'

'Did you go to the recital with your sister-in-law?'

'I didn't make any changes to our routine.'

'What were you planning to do?'

A vague wave of his hand.

'I don't know.'

'When did Lili discover the knife?'

'So it was her!' exclaimed Bellamy. 'I have wondered, from the beginning, what set you on the trail. I knew your wife was in the hospital where Lili died.'

'She sometimes talked in her delirium.'

'And she mentioned the knife?'

'The silver knife.'

'She was accusing me.'

He was taken aback, shocked.

'On the contrary, she defended you. She shouted to the nun that you shouldn't be arrested, that it was your wife who was the monster.'

'Oh!'

'She also uttered words which the nuns refused to repeat, filthy words, apparently.'

'That confirms what I told you.'

And, curious in spite of everything:

'Was it Sister Marie des Anges who alerted you?'

'Yes. I understood that in the car you and your sister-in-law were driving home in, she had found a clue, probably the knife.'

'That is correct.'

It was strange to see him examining his case with clarity, like a problem that had nothing to do with him, and yet Maigret was far from fooled, he could sense that the doctor was on the alert for the slightest sound in the house. It was as if he were counting the minutes during which he was still entitled to conduct himself as a man like any other.

'You see to what extent a ridiculous sentiment can take on importance. I had destroyed all the evidence. There was nothing, not the slightest clue against me. Nothing but that knife, which I had cleaned and put back in its place on my desk. Why? Out of habit, because I liked the shape of the handle. Perhaps too because I had always seen it there and I absently fiddled with it during my consultations.

'The next morning I saw it back in its place and I frowned, because it reminded me of a very particular gesture.

'I remember wrapping it in a handkerchief and putting it in my pocket. A little later, I took my car out. The knife was making me uncomfortable and I stuffed it in the little compartment on the right of the dashboard.

'I thought no more about it when, on the way back from La Roche-sur-Yon, Lili opened the compartment to take out some matches.

'She grabbed the handkerchief and opened it out.

'I can picture her, knife in hand, looking at me with horrified eyes. Of course she was thinking about the feet she had glimpsed the night before in my office. Maybe she knew more? Maybe she suspected her sister's affair?

'I lunged at her to take the knife away. Did she misinterpret my movement? I don't think so. She was obeying an irrational impulse. As I grabbed the knife by the blade, she let go and opened the door.

'I shouldn't have needed to kill Lili either. You believe that, don't you?'

'I believe that.'

'Afterwards, because of you, I had to defend myself.'

And Maigret said slowly:

'Defend what?'

'Not my life, you are aware of that. Not even my freedom. That's what I want you to understand, as I think only you are able to.

'Earlier, I gave up the fight, not because of the danger, not because I felt you were close to the truth, but because I realized that there would have to be other victims, that it would take too many.'

His lips were barely trembling now, but Maigret was no longer fooled.

'Including me.'

'Perhaps.'

'It wasn't mercy that stopped you.'

'No. I have no more mercy.'

True, the picture was inconsistent, but seeing him before his eyes, Maigret felt he was looking at a man who had been emptied of all his substance, completely gutted.

He came and went, drank, talked like a normal man, but there was no longer anything inside him, nothing but his mind which continued to work through strength of habit. Similarly, so it is said, the heads of those who have been decapitated continue to move their lips for a few minutes after the execution.

'What's the point?' he asked with a glance in the direction of the room he had locked so carefully earlier, whose key was in his pocket.

A scruple prompted him to keep as closely as possible to the truth.

'And yet . . . Listen . . . For the boy, I was almost within my rights . . . All I needed to do was catch them together, and any French jury would have acquitted me. In spite of that, I took upon myself the despicable task of getting rid of the body and lying. Why? I am going to tell you, ridiculous as it might seem to you: because I would have been arrested anyway, because I would have been sent to prison for a few weeks or a few days, because, for a few weeks or a few days, I *wouldn't have seen her*.'

His smile, this time, was chillingly wry and he poured himself another drink.

'That is the explanation. It was the same for the girl. You saw her here. I realized that you would find her, and question her, and that through her you would get to the truth, to the truth which for me, always meant the same thing: *not to see her . . .*'

His voice was choking. He still managed to say:
'That's all.'

But he wasn't able to swallow the drink he was holding. His throat was too tight. He remained motionless, frozen, and Maigret, for his part, stayed silent.

Cars drove past on the quayside. At any moment now, one of them would pull up in front of the house and they would hear the voice of the examining magistrate in the hall.

'If I hadn't been on holiday in Les Sables d'Olonne . . .' sighed Maigret at length.

The doctor nodded. They were both thinking of little Lucile.

'Admit that earlier, immediately after my telephone call—'

'No!'

The doctor was slowly regaining his composure.

'It was before. When I telephoned, I had already made up my mind . . .'

'You had thought of killing your wife and then yourself?'

'Romantic, isn't it? However, even the most intelligent of men has felt that temptation at least once in his lifetime.'

He put two fingers in the pocket of his waistcoat and pulled out a folded slip of paper which he held out to Maigret.

'It was for myself,' he sighed. 'You'd better destroy it right away, because accidents can easily happen. It's cyanide. Romantic as ever, you see! Admit that you were convinced that I wouldn't let myself be arrested alive.'

'Maybe.'

'And that still a few minutes ago, you wouldn't take your eyes off me . . .'

'That is true.'

'I had thought of it too, you see. You cannot imagine how thoroughly one thinks of everything in a situation like mine.'

He rose, picked up the decanter as if to pour another drink, but put it back down on the tray again.

'What's the point?' he said.

And, shrugging:

'That imbecile Alain will be here shortly. He won't believe either of us. He'll think we're taking him for a ride.'

He walked with halting steps.

'I'll live, you'll see! I'll do whatever it takes to live. It's absurd, but despite everything, I will keep hoping. As long as I am alive, she won't dare—'

He bit his lip and asked, in a different tone:

'Do you think I'll be manhandled, beaten, I don't know what?'

He spoke as a man of the world who had a horror of coming into contact with low life.

'Is it really filthy in the prisons? Will I have to share my cell with other convicts?'

Maigret stifled a smile. Bellamy caressed the leather bindings, the curios, with his eyes.

'I wonder what's keeping him.' Bellamy was growing impatient. 'It takes half an hour to drive over from La Roche-sur-Yon, without going fast . . .'

He walked over to the window. Even though it was lunchtime, there were pale shapes under the beach umbrellas and bathers in the waves that shimmered like fish scales.

'It's taking a long time,' he murmured.

Then:

'It will be horribly long!'

He turned towards the door, hesitant. He finally burst out:

'Say something! . . . You can see that . . . that—'

Just then there was a ring at the door which at last brought the long-awaited relief.

'I'm sorry . . . Please forgive me . . . That reminds me that you haven't had lunch . . .'

'I'm not hungry.'

Bellamy opened the door in a natural manner.

'Come upstairs, Alain.'

The magistrate could be heard grumbling as he climbed the stairs and made his way along the corridor.

'What's all this about? I was supposed to be having lunch with a friend. Someone you know, by the way. Castaing, from La Rochelle.'

A curt greeting for Maigret.

'What is happening that is so exceptional?'

'I killed young Duffieux and his sister.'

'What?'

'Ask the inspector.'

The magistrate shot Maigret a furious look.

'Just a moment! I don't like—'

'Listen, Alain. Calm down for a moment. I am tired. Monsieur Maigret will give you the details later. You'll find young Duffieux's body—'

A hesitation. Was there not yet time? With the arrival of Alain de Folletier, day-to-day life had just intruded into the library.

All he needed to do was deny it. There had been no witnesses to his conversation with Maigret. Could he not prevent his mother-in-law from talking, as he had prevented the others?

A few more words and it would be too late.

He uttered those words in such a detached voice that he sounded as if he were explaining some finer points of architecture.

'Before Les Sables d'Olonne had running water, we had

a cistern on the roof. It was filled using a hand pump, to supply water to the bathrooms. The cistern is still there. That's where the body is.

'As for the knife, I fear it will never be recovered. I threw it in a sewer. Come over here. Look to the left, in the direction of the pines. You see where the surface of the water is ruffled? That's where the main pipe runs before it empties out beyond the headland . . . Would you like a drink, Alain?'

'Listen . . .'

'For goodness' sake! I don't know how these things usually happen. I confess I'm horrified at the idea of being handcuffed. You will take me in your car. Once we're at La Roche, you can question me if you must. However, I'd prefer we did this another day. You will drive me to prison yourself . . .'

Once again, he addressed Maigret.

'Can one take any personal belongings?'

He was joking and at the same time he had to rest his hand on the table.

'Hurry, Alain.'

And Maigret came to his rescue:

'It would be best to do as he asks.'

They still had to go along the corridor, past a white door, Maigret bringing up the rear.

Bellamy walked with rapid steps and, instead of pausing, he speeded up as he passed his wife's door. He did not even look at it. He walked straight ahead, down the stairs and stopped, surprised himself, in front of the coat stand on which there were several of his hats.

He was wearing navy blue. He selected a pearl-grey hat and was unable to decide whether to take some gloves.

Francis had rushed up to open the door.

It was the most ordinary of departures, as if he were setting out for a stroll. A huge oblong of sunlight fell on the hall floor, making the pale marble gleam. The house had an indefinable smell of cleanliness and comfort.

In the doorway, Philippe Bellamy paused, hesitant. The magistrate's taxi was parked by the kerb. People were walking past. Snatches of conversation could be heard.

'Are you coming with us, Monsieur Maigret?'

Maigret shook his head.

Then the doctor delved into his pocket. Wordlessly, without looking at Maigret, he held something out to him and rapidly covered the few metres to the car.

You could tell that the magistrate, finally rid of Maigret, was preparing, as he settled into the seat, to rail against this whole business.

The engine was running. The car glided over the asphalt. A face appeared fleetingly, just as it was about to turn off, two feverish eyes stared at the person who had remained behind.

Francis, seeing Maigret standing on the doorstep, did not dare shut the door again. And in fact Maigret did go back into the house, looking at the little key that Bellamy had slipped into his hand, the key to the room with closed curtains where the air quivered with the regular breathing of a slumbering woman.

INSPECTOR MAIGRET

THE GRAND BANKS CAFÉ

GEORGES SIMENON

It was indeed a photo, a picture of a woman. But the face was completely hidden, scribbled all over in red ink. Someone had tried to obliterate the head, someone very angry. The pen had bitten into the paper. There were so many criss-crossed lines that not a single square millimetre had been left visible.

Captain Fallut's last voyage is shrouded in silence. To discover the truth about this doomed expedition, Maigret enters a remote, murky world of men on the margins of society; where fierce loyalties hide sordid affairs.

Translated by David Coward

INSPECTOR MAIGRET

OTHER TITLES IN THE SERIES

THE MADMAN OF BERGERAC
GEORGES SIMENON

'He recalled his travelling companion's agitated sleep – was it really sleep?
– his sighs and his sobbing.

Then two dangling legs, the patent leather shoes and hand-knitted socks.'

A distressed passenger leaps off a night train and vanishes into the woods. Maigret, on his way to a well-earned break in the Dordogne, is soon plunged into the pursuit of a madman, hiding amongst the seemingly respectable citizens of Bergerac.

Translated by Ros Schwartz

OTHER TITLES IN THE SERIES

And more to follow